WITHDRAWN FROM STOCK
DUBLIN CITY PUBLIC LIBRARIES

Tom Davis was six years old on the outbreak of World War Two, and *Race You to the Ragman!* closely follows his own experiences. After leaving school, Tom served a six-year apprenticeship in steel fabrication and worked in the construction industry until the 1980s. He has been writing the stories of Hardy Flower Thomas for several years and lives in Gravesend, Kent.

D1340864

RACE YOU TO THE RAGMAN!

Book One of the
Hardy Flower Thomas Series

Tom Davis

Book Guild Publishing
Sussex, England

First published in Great Britain in 2014 by
The Book Guild Ltd
The Werks
45 Church Road
Hove, BN3 2BE

Copyright © Tom Davis 2014

The right of Tom Davis to be identified as the author
of this work has been asserted by him in accordance with the
Copyright, Designs and Patents Act 1988.

All rights reserved. No part of this publication may be reproduced,
transmitted, or stored in a retrieval system, in any form or by any
means, without permission in writing from the publisher, nor be
otherwise circulated in any form of binding or cover other than
that in which it is published and without a similar condition being
imposed on the subsequent purchaser.

All characters in this publication are fictitious and any resemblance
to real people, alive or dead, is purely coincidental.

Typesetting in Sabon by
Keyboard Services, Luton, Bedfordshire

Printed in Great Britain by
CPI Group (UK) Ltd, Croydon, CR0 4YY

A catalogue record for this book is available from
The British Library.

ISBN 978 1 909984 14 1

Contents

Part I

1

Guy Fawkes' Night, 5 November 1936

The skinny kid munched greedily at the remains of a piece of sausage gripped in his grimy fingers. With him in the backyard was his friend Louie, a back-alley neighbour who had reclaimed that part of his father's discarded dinner of the previous day away from the fluttering starlings outside the kitchen door. He knew his friend would be pleased; in fact, 'Hardy Flower' Thomas felt quite jubilant that another kid had given him something. He was so excited as he ran up the garden and showed his mum his piece of cold sausage. In turn, the mother of six gave her skinny son, the fourth of her brood, a raw carrot to give to little Lou and told him to invite Louie to play in the garden.

The day was bright and cool as the two boys raced round the heap of rubbish piled up in the garden, as the rubbish was in every other garden in the vicinity. After their playful game of chase, the new friends lay down on the rough concrete path and looked up, past the clothes-line full of billowing sheets and pillowcases which to the two boys looked like a galleon in full sail. Higher up in the sky the clouds floated like piles of cotton wool trying to overtake each other. The rougher boy liked his new friend Lou from the back alley. Neither of them felt the cold nip in the air, simply because they were running about. In the kitchen doorway stood Hardy

Leabharlanna Poibli Chathair Baile Átha Cliath

Dublin City Public Libraries

Flower's twin sister, Daisy, who, hoping that she might play with the two boys, waited patiently with her big brown eyes wide open. Little Daisy waited in vain.

Like most little lads of three years of age, Hardy Flower didn't want to go to bed that night, especially as something different and exciting was going to happen; after all, it was Guy Fawkes Night, something everybody was talking about though the three-year-old twins had no idea what it all meant. As soon as night-time and the darkness came the bonfires were lit in the gardens. The kids getting excited as they waved about tiny sparklers while others received a smack round the head for going too near to the fire. Some of the bigger boys tried to look grown up wearing their dads' cast-off greasy and torn working caps, as they scuffled round in boots or wellingtons much too big for them. The girls walked and pranced in the light of the fire and posed in their mums' hats, as they, too, scuffled about in cast-off high-heeled shoes, through the leaves and in and out of the mud.

The twin's three elder brothers were out doing what mischief twelve- and fourteen-year-old boys do on Guy Fawkes Night. Their eldest brother, Clifford, at sixteen years of age, was attending his Boys Brigade evening.

It had been at this time in November three years previously that Mr and Mrs Thomas had been overheard discussing the impending adoption of their recently born twins whom they could ill afford to keep. Young Clifford, who was of a Christian nature, was horrified to hear that adoption of the baby twins was being considered. So as not to lose his baby brother and sister to the rich but childless Mr and Mrs Faunch – whom the twins' father worked for as a spare-time gardener at their huge house – Clifford decided that he would leave school at thirteen, a year earlier than usual, and hand over his wages to Mrs Thomas to help her with the housekeeping.

All the kids and their mums and dads became excited when the baked potatoes were handed out. Hardy Flower and his sister Daisy objected vehemently when their eldest sister, Rose, was ordered by their stern father to 'Take those two to bed at once.' Rose pushed and shoved the twins up the stairs with threats of smacking them very hard, if they misbehaved. This was one of their mother's favourite threats, which, when she carried it out with quick swipes of her fat hand and her stinging wedding ring, made all of her six children hop about. And so it was 'up the wooden hills to Bedfordshire' – for the twins a term which meant the end of their day and peace and quiet for the adults.

Daisy and Hardy Flower were hastily put to bed and thought to be settled down. But when all became quiet indoors the boy jumped out of bed and crept to the window to see what all the flashes and bangs, bright lights and excitement, were all about. Daisy and Hardy Flower weren't the only children to be bundled off to bed because he could see lots of other kids being ushered or ordered back into their homes, and as he watched he wondered why the grown-up neighbours started to run to and fro with crates of beer and the men and the women laughed and giggled with each other as they touched each other or quickly kissed behind a shed or in the shadows. Hardy Flower stared through the window curiously until somebody came up behind him and slapped his legs. His sister Rose had whispered in a menacing tone:

'If you don't come away from the window, the bogeyman will get you. There he is!'

Rose pointed to the figure of the ugly grinning Guy Fawkes burning merrily on the bonfire. He was still grinning behind his painted mask when the sparks flared up as he disappeared into the flames. Hardy Flower was put back to bed but that whole night he was restless as he imagined the neighbourly mums and dads as they kissed and fondled in the shadowy places away from the fires. This would remain forever his first memory.

Hardy Flower's family moved from the house within the

next year owing to the walls in the bedrooms being infested with bugs which had bred over the years between the layers of wallpaper. At night the bugs came out of hiding to feast on the blood of whoever was asleep in the room. The family soon learnt that when bedbugs bite they puncture the skin and a lump comes up which gets very itchy. The more you scratched, the more the bites itched. The way the bugs were destroyed was quite upsetting for the children as the fat body lice were placed between two adult thumbnails and squashed with a loud crack. The twins would never forget the stink of the devoured blood as the shells cracked open quite loudly.

To prevent the bugs from climbing up on to the beds, the legs were stood in old fish-paste tins filled with paraffin or disinfectant. This, however, didn't always stop the bedbugs from feeding because they always ran up the wall and across the ceiling, sniffing out their victims then dropping softly on to an unsuspecting victim's face or arms searching for the nearest warm nook and cranny. The nasty little monsters were quick breeders as they multiplied in the most inaccessible places such as springs and joints of a bed. To get rid of the vermin, you had to hold a tin of disinfectant underneath the packed writhing mass while a candle flame or a piece of lighted newspaper was used to burn the offending bugs out. Eventually the house was fumigated throughout. It was more convenient for the poorer people to move to another house.

The next house move for the Thomas family was to the more respectable Park Road where the same problem existed. Fortunately, however, the Fumigation Department could be called in to get rid of the verminous creatures, leaving the house stinking for days on end – it's a wonder the Thomas family themselves survived. Hardy Flower would never see another bedbug until he opened up the huge old family bible belonging to his grandfather.

For the Thomas family life was very full. If a man had a job he had to work hard. If and when Mr Hardy Thomas had a day off, he enjoyed it. The three youngest of the Thomas family always went to afternoon Sunday school and once they were out of sight Mrs Flower Thomas dutifully took the *News of the World* up to Mr Thomas who was waiting hopefully in their bed. In September 1938 Daisy and Hardy Flower, who was rapidly becoming a brat of a boy, went to the infants school. Hardy Flower would splash through the puddles when it had been raining, kicking the neatly swept-up piles of leaves everywhere. Of course, it was a new adventure to the Thomas twins. After the first three days Daisy and Hardy Flower went to school on their own, holding each other's hand until they arrived at the school playground which had a high spiked railing fence surrounding the whole building.

The other children had become hostile because the cleaner kids' mums didn't encourage their offspring to talk to the less privileged children. There were many children whose mums went to the school either to take or bring their children home, but Daisy and Hardy Flower came from a family of nine and as they had not been mollycoddled or spoilt the twins quickly learnt to fend for themselves.

September 1938

For the first Christmas they had at school most of the first-year infants performed in the Christmas pantomime. Their first panto was *Snow White and the Seven Dwarfs* with Hardy Flower as one of the dwarfs. All the kids had to ask their mums to go and watch and encourage their 'starlets'. Hardy Flower's mum, Mrs Flower Thomas, sat in the front row but didn't recognise her little hero behind his cotton-wool beard. Hardy Flower wouldn't tell the other kids who his mum was because most of those kids of five had mums who were in their early twenties and slim; his mum was forty and fat. Hardy Flower didn't love his mum – not then.

After the Christmas panto and a visit from Father Christmas, Snow White and her seven dwarfs dashed off to show their mums their apple or orange and one-penny toy. It seemed to the twins, Hardy Flower and Daisy, that they only had oranges at Christmas time, but the twins were happy as their teacher told them that Father Christmas would call again soon. With that sweetener, it was out to play in the snow which was warmer than playing indoors at home.

After Christmas the twins went back to the tiny classroom and their tiny desks. It was after their first Christmas that the infants started 'Religious Instruction'.

During playtime the children stood in the cold playgrounds sucking ice-cold milk through straws. Some of the 'tots' had dainty little sandwiches or fairy cakes and biscuits. Hardy Flower always had bread and dripping from the Sunday roast – their mum told her twins that this was more 'grown up'. Hardy Flower often wondered why the other kids thought this was funny. Perhaps they were jealous because his lunch was wrapped in newspaper and the posh kids only had paper bags.

Back in the classroom the children settled down to do their colouring. Hardy Flower ate his coloured wax crayon when the teacher left the room. When the teacher returned, she had a little girl with her who was just starting school for the first time. The teacher stood in front of the class holding the little girl's hand.

'Quiet please, children. Now, Brenda dear, are there any children in the classroom who you might know?'

The little girl wore two large white bows of white ribbon on her two large bunches of jet-black hair. 'Little Brenda' looked at each of the children in turn and caught sight of her cousin Malcolm and very perkily answered:

'Yes, teacher, Malcolm is my cousin, and I would like to sit next to him.'

In between Malcolm and a little girl called Betty Peachy

was an empty chair and, although little Betty was a tiny little tot she was 'in love' and her sweetheart was Malcolm. Malcolm was quite unaware of Betty's love for him. There was no way that Betty wanted anybody to come between her and her sweetheart. When Brenda spoke, little Betty's big brown eyes blazed with fire as she stood up, banging her tiny fists down on to the desk top and stamping her tiny feet in anger. She shouted across to Brenda in a most adamant manner:

'You are not going to sit between Malcolm and me. So there.'

Tears of pure hatred ran down her cheeks as the kids listened in awe. Despite her outburst, the teacher ushered Brenda to the empty seat. Brenda was slightly bigger than either Betty or Malcolm and both moved their chairs to make room for her.

Brenda and Malcolm were happy cousins despite Brenda being the bossy one. The way little Betty kept her sweetheart Malcolm was by becoming Brenda's 'best friend'. This lasted until long after Brenda's infatuation for Malcolm was over. The two girls remained the best of friends and very often after the morning or afternoon playtime there would be two girls missing. A few minutes later they would appear in the doorway side by side, chanting: 'Please, teacher, we had to queue at the shop.' Hardy Flower was already in love with Brenda and his love would last another ten years.

Opposite the infants' school was an end-of-terrace house where the ground-floor front was a shop that sold 'everything' – which catered especially for the kids with their halfpennies or, if they were more fortunate, their old pennies. During their years at the Cecil Road School Betty and Brenda must surely have tried all sorts of goodies which 'Old Sterny', the Jewish shopkeeper, sold.

From time to time the 'nit nurse' visited the infants school and, if any of the kids were unfortunate enough to have nits, they were hastily ushered to the Headmistress's office where she always gave the cooty child a boiled sweet to suck. Afterwards the 'clean' kids and their mums had something to talk about. There were special combs for nits which were double-edged and referred to as 'the fine-toothed comb'. The fine-toothed comb took its toll as the nitty victims leant over a spread-out newspaper to have the nits raked out. Hopping and jumping in all directions, the nits tried to escape and the startled children wondered where they had all came from.

After being subjected to the double-edged comb, the sore-headed victims had their head and hair scrubbed with a black tarry soap named Durbac. Afterwards, the newspaper was rapidly rolled up and burnt on the school caretaker's coke stove.

'I'm glad I'm not a dog,' thought Hardy Flower. 'They're running alive and they stink.'

Hardy Flower was almost six years old when he was admitted into the local hospital to have his tonsils removed. He was sitting in his cot when a visiting mum came over to him and asked: 'Haven't you got any toys to play with, dear?' Although it was quite obvious that the skinny, rough-looking kid hadn't got any toys, the lady went to another bed and spoke to her son, who nodded his head in agreement to her suggestion. The lady, Mrs Tickner, asked her son, John, whether he would mind if Hardy Flower played with his clockwork van on which were seated the Walt Disney characters. Hardy Flower loved the toy and cried his eyes out when it was time for his new friend John to go home and for the toy to go home with him.

After the removal of his tonsils, Hardy Flower was laid back in his cot still under the anaesthetic. It was dark when the young boy came to and his throat felt tight and burning as if it was on fire. In the middle of the ward was a table on which stood a jug of water and a glass. Moonlight shone right on to the throat-quenching liquid. Hardy Flower decided to get to the water so that he could cool his raging throat.

But first he had to climb over the side of his cot, which proved quite easy for a rough and adventurous kid.

As he padded over to the table, it didn't occur to him how he would get back into his cot. Now minus his tonsils, Hardy Flower crawled to the table and climbed on to a chair, reaching up for the water jug. However, just as his fingers gripped the handle he felt the back of his night-shirt lifted and a stinging slap across his bare bottom. Of course, the five-year-old adventurer started to cry – or croak through his sore throat – as the nurse screamed out: 'You naughty child! What are you doing out of your cot?'

As if a young child could give a reasonable explanation! Hardy Flower croaked again, and as he was laid back into his cot he tried to tell the nurse that his throat was hurting him and that he would like a drink of water.

But his hoarse bleatings went unheeded as he received another slap from the heavy-handed nurse. 'Go to sleep,' she snarled. 'You'll never get better if you run around the ward in your night-shirt. Ugh! Disgusting boy!'

To the stiff and well-starched night nurse, the small and underfed patient looked like a home-made ragdoll with no stuffing, a scrawny neck and all head.

As the five-year-old patient lay there looking at the water jug and wondering why the burning lump in his throat felt worse, he imagined he could see Mickey Mouse and Minnie Mouse pointing to him from inside their tin van, but it was only a dream.

Two days later John Tickner came into the ward to see him and to give Hardy Flower a toy to keep in place of the Walt Disney van. Hardy Flower cherished the roughly carved wooden soldier for years and years, forever thinking, 'I'll be a soldier one day!' And so he would.

The Thomas twins were often referred to at school and in the adjoining roads where they lived as the 'poor kids from the rough family'. They possessed just one set of clothes compared with the several changes the other kids wore each week. There were no smelly or dirty clothes for those 'posh kids'! The Thomas family's lack of money stuck out like a sore thumb and very often several of the more privileged children slyly asked Daisy or her brother for a piece of their thick chunks of bread smeared with jam, lard or dripping. Not content with a hunk of the twins' doorstep slices of bread, the children also expected a piece of the newspaper wrapping to carry it away in. Hardy Flower thought they wanted to swap theirs for his, but then the 'posh brats' would just run away with their prize.

Should any of the kids have a halfpenny or a one-penny piece, it was always spent in 'Old Sterny's' on a halfpenny Oxo cube or a packet of soup powder for one penny while a threepenny piece (a 'thruppenny joey') would buy a whole 'Edward's' soup block. Very often, if one of the poorer kids couldn't scrounge a lick, they'd do their utmost to catch a 'nit' and be awarded a boiled sweet by the Headmistress. The under-privileged and poorer kids outnumbered the posh children at the school by three to one.

Very often a rag-and-bone man waited outside the school gates with a huge suitcase full of toys and books or anything which kids wanted. In exchange, the only thing the hawker asked for the toys was bundles of rags. Most of the kids would dash home to ask their mums for any old clothes and rags, which they'd then swap for the colourful toys.

'Come on. Race you to the ragman!' Hardy Flower would shout to his sister, having given himself several yards' start. And they'd race to the brightly coloured pile of toys and watch as the other kids walked away with the toys of their choice. The twins Daisy and Hardy Flower Thomas already had their bundle of rags – they were wearing them.

2

Outbreak of Second World War, 1939, and First Evacuation

Early on in the war in 1940 urban-dwelling civilians pasted strips of gummed paper across their window panes and pulled down large roller blinds at night to prevent any light from shining out. Then heavy curtains were draped across the inside of the windows ensuring that any light from inside couldn't be seen from the outside. The strips of sticky paper helped to prevent the fragmented glass from flying about when the bombs exploded. England was at war with Germany and being bombed daily from the air. It was the start of the Battle of Britain. And for some children it was the time of their lives. But not for the Thomas twins, Hardy Flower and Daisy.

During the dark evenings the Air Raid Precaution teams patrolled the streets looking for fires or any exposed lights which might be shining through windows. In the event of the wardens finding any lights showing, they would bawl out with a resounding roar? 'Put those lights out!' Any light shining through a window apparently shone up into the night sky where the German Luftwaffe might be guided by it and aim their bombs at it. As the bombers flew over, a siren wailed making everybody dive for cover. When war was declared in 1939 everybody dug a trench across their gardens and well away from the house as if preparing for trench warfare. The trenches were about seven feet deep and three feet wide and stretched from one end of a road to the other. Each garden's trench was joined together as a convenience for ambulances. As the German bombers flew over, whole families stood in the trenches looking up, counting the aeroplanes and watching the shells burst high up in the sky, seconds later, razor-sharp shards of hot shrapnel would hit the ground with a thud. When an aeroplane was hit, the crew would jump out and drift off in their parachutes as the bomber went crashing to the ground, sometimes killing many people.

The squadrons of enemy bombers followed the line of the River Thames, heading for London to bomb the various docks, which were a hive of industry during the days of conflict. The aerial dog fights became more frequent, with several air-raids each day, which caused parents to become very concerned about their children. In late 1939 the Government decided that children who lived in the heavily bombed areas of south-east England should be evacuated if the parents so wished. But first everybody had to be issued with gas masks, which they had to carry around with them at all times. The gas mask was carried in a cardboard box attached to a piece of string which was slung over the shoulder. The more affluent were able to have leather outer covers to suit their taste. Everybody was convinced that they would all be gassed by the German bombers who were already dropping phosphorous bombs which set light to everything when they exploded. They also dropped 'Butterfly' bombs which looked like giant butterflies. When they were touched they exploded, killing or maiming anybody who was within the blast. Another scare was that poisoned sweets were being dropped to kill young children. That and other frightening aspects of the war convinced many parents to evacuate their children to various places of safety.

Daisy and Hardy Flower were destined to go to Windsor, and on 3 September 1939 with hundreds of other children they stood on the platform of Gravesend Railway Station with large parcel labels tied to their coat collars on which was written 'WINDSOR'. As they were just six years old, their father went with them to the railway station to see them off. Mr and Mrs Thomas had convinced their twins that they were going on a long holiday, quite unaware of the type of family their two unsuspecting children were going to be fostered out to – for just over £1 a week for two children's board and lodging.

The huge steam locomotive whistled loud and shrill as it came to a screeching stop at the railway station. The train had been laid on specially for the evacuees who were travelling from Gravesend to Windsor, changing trains in London. Most children carried a suitcase of sorts containing their clothes and toiletries, but for the Thomas twins it was a paper carrier bag containing a towel and a piece of torn towel for a face flannel with an assortment of soap scraps. Neither of the twins possessed a toothbrush or a comb. Over their shoulder they carried their gas masks in a cardboard box with a string shoulder support. And both of them held, in their other hand, a paper bag containing the remains of two ounces of pear drops. A treat for the twins to go away on holiday with.

Like many other children, the twins wouldn't remember very much about their evacuation except that after their arrival they spent all day waiting to be chosen or picked out to be fostered. Like two skinny and underfed waifs, they stood alone in the town hall, Daisy slightly pigeon-toed and with her big brown eyes glistening tears in anticipation. Hardy Flower stood holding her hand, his slightly smaller brown eyes darting here and there suspiciously when he thought a bargain-hunter had chosen his sister. Perhaps his jug-like ears, on his large cropped head, supported by a very skinny and tide-marked neck which made him look like a starving alley cat, with one corner of his mouth turned down slightly in a seemingly mocking sneer, did nothing to enhance the six-year-old twins appearance. Neither of them wore socks on their feet, just the common leather sandals of that era. A cotton dress and knickers for the girl and short-legged unlined trousers for him – still damp from wetting his bed the night before – with a thin button neck jersey. No underwear for him and no coat for either of them. Every few seconds they would glance at each other as some short and fat, long and thin, miserable or happy, boisterous or quiet, and some hopefully 'on to a good thing' prospective child carer, sized up the 'away from home alone' kids.

Eventually, they dared to sit down simply because there was nobody else about; every single child had been picked out and taken away, it was quite obvious that nobody had wanted to be a foster parent to a pair of twins. They sat there, both trying to look brave for the other as they blinked back the tears. Then suddenly they heard a loud braying voice:

'Eow! Ay say! Where is everyone? Oh deah, is this all that there is left? These two scrawny children on this seat? Why on earth are they wearing those huge brown parcel labels pinned to their clo'thing – did they arrive by post!?'

The posh-sounding lady peered closely at Hardy Flower and his sister Daisy, adding:

'May God, they are so grubby-looking too!'

It was almost fourteen hours since the twins had left home for the first time in their life, so their untidy state was inevitable.

The posh lady took them with disdain written right across her over-decorated face. It was the twins or nothing and she didn't want the neighbours to think she wasn't doing her bit for the poor evacuees from the other side of London. And she would get twice the amount of evacuees allowance from the government. The 'grubby-looking' twins would look even grubbier and more waifish, when they were taken out of her care several months later.

The lady's home was a very clean house which always

smelled of perfumed soap. Inside the spotless house and outside in the lawned garden everything was spic and span, including the posh lady's two children. The surrounding neighbours were sympathetic and friendly towards the twins who thought how nice it was to be billeted so near to Windsor Castle where they hoped they might see the King.

On a fine summer evening during the first week there, Daisy and Hardy Flower were playing chase in the garden when suddenly they were ordered straight to their bedroom. The twins had always stayed up at home until it got dark and they thought they would be allowed the same privilege at Windsor with the children of the house. But it was not to be because they were ordered to go immediately to bed while the other two children played nicely and romped with their pedigree Afghan hound around the smartly lawned garden.

'Go to bed immediately!' snarled the twins new spic-and-span foster mother. 'And don't you dare touch the furniture or the wallpaper with your grimy hands. Go on! Wash yourselves in the bathroom and use your own face flannels and towels – ugh! God! How on earth did I get these two skinny brats? It makes me wonder what I might catch from them?' It was as if Hardy Flower and Daisy were urchins from the gutters of Oliver Twist's London.

In the pink-and-blue marble and glass bathroom the twins' tattered and grubby towels and facecloths lay on a piece of brown paper on the floor in the corner where they had been dropped earlier that week. Not for them a pink-and-blue fluffy towel. Not for them Knight's Castile perfumed soap; only remnant of Sunlight carbolic laundry scrubbing soap. Neither did they have a toothbrush or a comb.

Up to their bedroom the twins sadly shuffled, out of the way. In the spare and sparse bedroom Hardy Flower leapt up on to the bed to look though the window and across the distant fields towards Windsor Castle which was flying the

17

Union Jack on top of one of the towers. As the boy gazed though the window somebody moved in the garden below him, and there, looking up at him was the lady of the house who seemed to be waving. So, being a friendly little soul, he smiled and waved back. His sunny nature couldn't understand the sudden vicious look which had come over her face as she suddenly turned and marched into the house. Sad and despondent he continued to gaze at the Union Jack until suddenly, wallop! – something hit his head, and his head hit the window. Instead of seeing the flag, he saw stars. The lady who a moment before had seemed so nice was screaming at Hardy Flower.

'Ai ordered you to bed! And when ai say ge'ow to bed, Ai mean ge'ow to bed! And de'own't you ever dare to defy me again!'

As she spoke, the knuckles of her beautifully manicured fingers knocked their meaning into the boy's cropped head while, at his side, his twin sister Daisy sat holding back the dam of tears in her saucer-like eyes. Neither of them dared to blink or swallow as, under the malevolent gaze of their irate foster mother, they hastily stepped out of their lower garments, jumped into bed and cowered beneath their solitary blanket.

The lady of the house had sounded so posh and spoke so nicely at first that Hardy Flower thought she must be the Queen – popped over from Windsor Castle. The 'Queen' stormed out of the bedroom, locking the door behind her. There would be no tea or supper for the twins that day.

Things didn't turn out to be much better at their new school. They were ignored or shoved aside: 'Don't come near me, I don't want evacuees' fleas!' or 'Stay away from us, you smelly kids!' Quick digs, spiteful slaps and crafty kicks kept the twins at a distance from the kids who seemed to have a good life.

On their way 'home' from school one afternoon, the twins

were walking along a country lane when they came across a unit of soldiers who had stopped for a smoke. The soldiers spoke to the children, and one of them who came from the twins' home county, gave them a box of Liquorice All-Sorts. The soldiers were kind and sympathetic to the twins – in all probability some of their children were evacuees also.

When they arrived back at the house, their foster mother's mother was there trying on some clothes, so the twins were hurriedly ushered out of the room though not before their 'carer' had relieved them of the box of Liquorice All-Sorts. The old lady stood there in a huge pair of knee-length knickers, held up by wide thick elastic at her waist. The lady was enormously fat and as the twins got the 'bum's rush' through the door Hardy Flower noticed that she was already scoffing the soldier's gift.

Left on their own at school, the twins went deeper and deeper into their shell, while back at the house they continued to fend for themselves. The only thing which they weren't required to do was cook their own food as scant as it was. As the weeks went by, their bodies became grimier and grimier until the only clean part of them was their hands, and that was only because they had to put them into the buckets of hot soda water they used to scrub their bedroom. Her own two children were not allowed to associate with the twins at any time, while the man of the house completely ignored them.

After Hardy Flower and Daisy had been away for about four months, there came a Christmas which the twins would never forget. The lady of the house wanted just her and her family at home for Christmas, so to make things easier the twins were allowed to have their very own Christmas and Boxing Day, locked in the privacy of their bleak, sparse bedroom as they listened to the festive joy and glee of their foster family downstairs. Not yet able to read, the twins could only look at the pictures on their mum and dad's Christmas card. Not yet seven years of age, they didn't question the whys and wherefores of their vastly changed life.

Home for the Blitz

It wasn't very long after Christmas when Mr Hardy Thomas and Mrs Flower Thomas decided that the twins should return home. The lonely children were overjoyed to see their dad again, especially when they were told that he was taking them back to Gravesend with him – despite the heavy bombing that the town was subjected to both day and night – the Blitz on London had started. The twins were overjoyed to be going home again, though they would leave home again three more times before they were twelve years of age.

Mr Hardy Thomas and his twins travelled back home to Gravesend on the Sunday, and on Monday morning the twins were back at their school desks at Cecil Road Infants School. The next weekend would be Easter 1940.

At home and at school they were considered to be the 'rough-and-ready ragamuffin kids' but they did at least get a weekly bath. After the four months of neglect at Windsor, Hardy Flower and Daisy had to have Vaseline rubbed into their bodies everyday to loosen the grimed-in dirt.

'But,' said their mum, Mrs Flower Thomas, 'it's done them good. I want my kids to be rough and ready!'

For what?

Very soon after their return home everybody became very busy filling in the never-ending trenches which had been dug for them to dive into when the siren wailed its eerie warning. It was a good opportunity for everybody to get rid of any old junk which they wanted to get rid of such as old bike frames, worn-out tin baths, old bedsteads and prams. Everything was dumped into the trench, which had suddenly become obsolete. Two enterprising ministers of the wartime government

– namely Anderson and Morrison – had decided that every home should have an air-raid shelter. Instead of a trench, each household was given the choice of either an Anderson shelter or a Morrison shelter.

The Anderson shelter was designed to stand half buried in the garden but situated well away from the house, and the only indication that it was there was a huge hump in the ground. It was made of corrugated steel, was six feet long and had an arched roof. Inside were a number of bunk beds on each side. The more privileged families kept a water-tight cupboard with life's necessities stored in it. Some shelters had a breather tube to keep the air circulating and to help prevent condensation, the more forward-thinking made simple duckboards to cover the damp or flooded earth floors.

The Morrison shelter was a huge steel 'dining-room table' that resembled a cage. Inside, under its steel-plated top, was room to make up four family beds. Mr Hardy Thomas decided that the family would be safer halfway down the garden in their iron cave. The 'iron cave' was erected in a large hole. Then, once it was in position, the loose soil was thrown back round the outsides and over the top and packed in hard. A very small entrance at one end was just large enough for a body to crawl through. Some people were fortunate enough to build a wooden door which kept the draughts out and they'd keep a bunk made up ready to sleep in, with a paraffin stove to keep them warm and the interior dry. But for the Thomas family, instead of a door, there was an empty coal sack hanging down with two house bricks to hold it in place. When the family needed to use the air-raid shelter quickly, they dived into it and sat on a blanket, though only if they had managed to grab one from their bed. The 'better orf' people had several blankets, vacuum flasks and boxes of biscuits which they kept in the shelters as a stand-by for when there were extra-long air-raids, or should they be entombed by debris from bomb blasts. The only biscuits the

21

Thomas twins ever saw were to the side of their mum's early-morning cup of tea.

Whenever the air-raid siren wailed everybody had to hurry to the nearest shelter immediately and stay there until the 'all-clear' sounded. Sometimes Daisy and Hardy Flower would sit and play in the shelter or invite other kids in to play. During the air-raids they listened to the bombs whistling down and they would hear the explosions. On some occasions, they would try and look up with their heads out of the door and try to count the German bombers. There seemed to be hundreds and hundreds of them. When Hardy Flower went to bed at night he took a dinner knife with him and hid it under his pillow: 'To kill the Germans if they landed.'

The town and outer districts each had their 'salvage' gangs, who called round to collect any old junk to be recycled to make airplanes, ships, bombs and anything which would help the war effort. Mrs Flower Hardy gave some old aluminium saucepans for salvage and the next day, as a few airplanes flew overhead, Hardy Flower could see the sun's rays being reflected back from the shiny fuselages.

'Mum! Mum!' he shouted. 'There goes our saucepans!'

After the air-raids the kids always went looking for shrapnel, the fragmented chunks of shells that fell out of the sky. Unfortunately, many people were killed by the jagged lumps of red-hot metal just before they hit the ground. Hardy Flower made a collection of the lethal scrap, which he swapped for this and that – mainly sweets. A thrilling spectacle witnessed by thousands over the River Thames several times was to see the pilots floating down on their parachutes – it wasn't very pleasant for them, of course, especially when their aircraft had been blasted out of the sky. Many of the pilots would land in the River Thames. After he'd seen the fighter pilots parachuting from their blazing aircraft, Hardy Flower became adventurous. 'If they can do it, then so can I!'

Hardy Flower's very first parachute – and there would be

real ones for him later – was made from brown wrapping paper three feet square, with a piece of string tied on each corner. The ends of the string he tied to a butcher's hook which he pushed through the rough wool of the collar on his jersey. His airplane exit was the top bedroom windowsill, and many many times the would-be parachutist sat on the window ledge twenty feet above the concrete path, wanting to jump, though he never did. The adventurous kid decided there and then that one day he would participate in parachute jumping.

Often on a summer's day, Hardy Flower defended his castle from the top of the air-raid shelter armed with his sword made from somebody's gladioli fronds or from the sharp spiky leaves of an iris plant, and with his bow and arrow slung over his shoulder the pint-sized warrior did battle with his enemies who had been attacking his castle all morning. He'd repel them, too, with cannon balls which were handfuls of pebbles. With a screech and a lot of shrieking, his enemy sister Daisy was routed as she went running up the garden path, retreating to the safety of the kitchen. The rough-neck knight, Sir Lancelot Hardy Flower, had won the battle, though his little war was not yet finished. Daisy was crying because he had hit her behind the ear with a pebble cannon ball. The twins' distraught mother, Mrs Flower Thomas, was shouting her lungs out at him. 'You little bugger!' which she emphasised with a swipe of her knuckles and wedding ring to the back of his head.

'Daisy is going to pay for that!' Hardy Flower snarled in his humiliation as the siren started to wail.

Within seconds the sky was full of droning bombers high in the sky, all heading up-river towards Tilbury Docks and London. As the anti-aircraft guns blazed away to try and shoot them down, Hardy Flower's 'little war' was postponed for the duration of the air-raid.

After the German bombers had passed over the industrial

areas of Gravesend and Northfleet the 'all-clear' sounded, then everybody would stop whatever they were doing to hear the bombs exploding on Tilbury and Dagenham Docks. It was time for the miniature knight to continue with his next battle, but for the next battle Hardy Flower allowed Daisy to be the 'King' and the new 'defender' of his castle, hoping it might prevent him from getting a good hiding from their fraught and exasperated mum. The young knight errant retreated to behind the pear tree, just in case Daisy used his store of pebbles for cannon balls or hand grenades, and as another precaution he put his tin helmet on because he was about to charge the ramparts. But his mum's enamelled kitchen colander was quite wobbly on his head, so he secured it on with a piece of string threaded through two holes and tied with a bow under his chin.

Once more the sirens sounded, indicating that the German bombers had finished their raid on London and were on their way back to the Reich, but by the time they reached the skies over north-east Kent the Royal Air Force reception committee was waiting to greet the Nazis high in the sky. Once again, the Gravesendians watched as the German Messerschmitts and English Spitfires started their wheeling and diving. To the kids and adults alike, it was truly a sight to behold.

As Mrs Thomas, Daisy and Rose watched, the next-door neighbour suddenly came running down the garden path shouting.

'Take cover! Take cover! We're being machine-gunned!'

Through the warm summer air could be heard a distant 'brrr-brrr-brrr-brrr'. The family ran indoors but were stopped in their tracks when Mrs Thomas shouted:

'That's not machine guns! It's that little bugger playing on my treadle sewing machine!'

The rise and fall of the needle going through the sewing block did indeed sound similar to the distant machine guns being fired high in the sky. The adults found it very amusing at the time. All through the Blitz the sense of humour was unequalled.

Very often, when nobody was about, Hardy Flower crept into the room where the sewing machine stood. The skinny boy could just about stand on the treadle underneath the worktop, with his hands outstretched and holding on to the wrought-ironwork legs at each end. He would treadle so fast that he couldn't stop, causing the cottons and bobbins to become entangled and the needle to snap. Once again, he found himself dragged out by his ear and held suspended on his tiptoes with his head on one side. A sound thrashing with ringed fingers across the back of his thighs was painful, but even worse was when the young victim was suspended by his ear – in the grip of a fat thumb and forefinger.

Mr Hardy Thomas, the twins' father, had been through one war, lived in the trenches, had 'gone over the top' as an infantryman, and been wounded, but in 1940 he had a reserved occupation. Nonetheless, he was keen to do his bit. Mr Hardy Thomas had two allotment gardens as well as his own back garden due to the 'Dig for Victory!' campaign, the posters for which were displayed on walls and fences. There was a shortage of food and people were encouraged to grow their own vegetables. The huge poster displayed a working-class man digging in a garden, and Hardy Flower thought the man digging in the picture was his dad. It really was necessary for a family to grow their own vegetables and Hardy Flower liked to help his dad in the garden.

Food was so scarce that sometimes Hardy Flower, the weakest and hungriest of the twins, would arrive home from school at lunchtime and end up going to the local park to play because there was nothing to eat. Everybody was issued with a ration book for food and one for clothes. A person could only have so much food for each week and limited clothes for a year. If they were lucky, a weekly ration would amount to one egg, one quarter-pound of sugar, one ounce of cheese, one slice of bacon, four ounces of butter and a few ounces of meat. The sweet ration was three-quarters of a pound per month. The sweet ration always started on a Monday, but the sweet-shop owners usually opened on a Sunday until noon for people to have a treat, although it was against the law to open a shop on a Sunday.

One time at school during religious instruction the teacher told the class how the Lord created the world in six days and rested on the seventh day which was called the Sabbath. He then asked:

'You, boy!' He pointed at Hardy Flower. 'What is the first day of the week?'

The schoolboy answered: 'Monday is, sir.'

'And how do you know that, boy?' bawled the teacher.

Hardy Flower answered with his best 'amart Alec' sneer.

'Because the sweet coupons start on a Monday!'

Straight away the class laughed as the teacher knuckled the back of the cheeky boy's head, hissing.

'Don't be clever, boy! Stay behind after school and write out two hundred lines: "I, Hardy Flower Thomas, shalt not make a mockery of my class teacher!" Correctly punctuated, if you please, Hardy Flower Thomas!'

He was, in fact, the best teacher the boy ever had.

Fish and chips were very cheap during the war. A piece of fried cod was sixpence and a portion of chips two pence. When the twins' parents had fish and chips for supper it was always after the twins had gone to bed earlier than usual. But when the twins came downstairs in the morning the smell of fish and chips still lingered, and on some occasions when they were playing on the floor one of them might discover a cold chip which had been dropped the night before. They always broke it in halves and shared it because they were always hungry.

Like a ritual, the kids had a regular medical examination

26

at the school, and the medical officers ordered that Daisy and her twin brother should be allowed two free dinners each day until further notice, because they were suffering from malnutrition. It was this that may well have accounted for Hardy Flower's 'dumping it down the throat syndrome', which lasted for many years. This habit may in turn have caused him to suffer with stomach ulcers and acute indigestion, both of which he found extremely painful. The ulcers took their toll when he reached twelve years of age, caused by a combination of insecurity and scoffing anything edible. On the too many occasions when Hardy Flower was hungry he'd steal and scoff lots of raw runner beans, which eventually made him vomit. Many times when he was hungry he'd steal and eat dog biscuits, which he found extremely hard. The forever hungry boy assumed that all kids ate dog biscuits! because he thought they were very tasty.

The food situation in the Thomas household became quite bad because Mrs Flower Thomas couldn't handle the rations or the money, so she decided that everybody should dispose of their own rations as they liked. Thus, Hardy Flower's piece of cheese went in one gulp. The butter ration meant one good spread over one slice of bread while the one egg and one slice of bacon was always saved for Sunday morning breakfast. In between those luxuries the family 'enjoyed' meat dishes made from sixpenny-worth of bones from the butcher's. Sometimes it was called soup and sometimes it was called broth, but when it got too thin and watery an Oxo cube was added to make it a 'stew'.

A treat for the family, if there was sixpence to spare, would be fresh herrings or bloaters for their dinner. If the fishing boats had been given a rough time in the English Channel by the Luftwaffe, then it was back to bread and jam, lard or dripping fat.

3

Off to Gloucester for a Second Holiday with Granny and Gramps

During 1940 the German air-raids became very intense, and parents were again encouraged to evacuate their children to safer areas well away from the bombs and shrapnel which fell daily – on some occasions, several times a day. Every so often, train loads of children would be off to all points of the compass in and around England and away from the south-east. Some children were lucky enough to go further abroad to even safer areas, such as Canada and the USA.

Flower and Hardy Thomas, the twins' parents, once again decided that Daisy and Hardy Flower should, along with their sister Rose, go away. But this time they would go to stay with their gran and Gramps Thomas, who lived in a country village in Gloucestershire.

The twins were two or three months off being seven years old, and Rose, their eldest sister, was twelve or thirteen years old. Their Gran and Gramps were kind people, and Gramps's mother (the twins' great-grandmother) lived down a little country lane at the end of which stood a very old castle – hence the name, Castle Lane. Her cottage was a two-up-and-two-down and covered with deep-red roses. On the twins' last visit a photograph had been taken including four generations of the family.

Gran and Gramps lived in a tiny village called Whitminster

on the old Bristol road. The old Whitminster village was about seven miles west of Bristol. Gran and Gramps's house was very old and spooky, as well as being cold and damp. The house name was Hillview and the house still stands to this day. Originally, the owners had servants, who lived in their own quarters at the side of the house, but at the turn of the century the connecting door was locked and the key lost, and over the many years many coats of paint had covered the key hole.

Hardy Flower loved the food at Whitminster. There was always fresh farm bread delivered each day (there was no such thing as 'sliced bread'). The butter, milk and Cheddar cheeses were also delivered straight from the farms. Sometimes their Uncle Tom brought it home from the farm, where he worked as a cowman. According to the season, there was always lots of fruit, which Gran made her jams with, all neatly placed on the cold shelves of the walk-in and walk-round pantry. In those days there was no need for refrigerators as the pantry shelves were made of thick marble on which stood the fresh pails of milk and urns of fresh spring water. The farmhands delivered the fresh cow's milk in huge churns on the back of a horse and cart, delivered to the cottage in a bucket and scooped out with a jug, and the forever hungry Hardy Flower often sneaked into the pantry to sip the cool milk and take a piece of cheese rind on his way out.

While they lived with their Gran, Rose took care of the twins, which meant she had to make sure that they were washed and dressed before she took them to school. Rose was also very comforting to the twins when they cried for their parents, which was very often. Away from their home again, they attended the village school, which was no bigger than a two-bedroom cottage. The headmaster was a Mr Bullock and the lady teacher, Miss Dance.

The children enjoyed the summer in the countryside. On one occasion, Hardy Flower watched two aeroplanes very high in the sky engaged in aerial combat. The English and German fighter pilots ducked and weaved at the same time as the young boy's fingers were engaged in picking his nose. He was so engrossed and excited as he watched the vapour trails high in the sky that his frantic groping up his nostrils made his nose bleed. Uncle Tom, who also lived with their Gran, laughingly called Hardy Flower 'a dirty little bugger'. 'That will teach you to leave your bloody nose alone!' he added.

Gramps and Uncle Tom grew enough vegetables and potatoes in the garden to last through the winter. Hardy Flower loved the smell of the broad beans and the fine country air. His Gran very often cooked him tasty snacks that he would never forget – fried bacon and a fried pig's ear with fried new potatoes complete with a fried duck's egg, all of which he smothered with HP sauce. To finish off, the forever hungry boy cleaned his plate off with a crust from a fresh, warm cottage loaf.

Hardy Flower wandered alone along the canal banks to collect moorhens' eggs, but only one from each nest. These his Gran fried for his tea. At first, the doubtful kid thought the old lady would moan at him for taking them, but it was a recognised practice in the country to eat moorhens' eggs. Hardy Flower's intention was to save them and take them home for his parents – whenever that would be!

Before the twins had gone to Windsor, a next-door neighbour had bought Hardy Flower a three-piece suit, which included a waistcoat, for his sixth birthday. Thankfully for him he didn't have to wear it very often. But he had to take it to Gloucester where he had to wear it to Sunday school.

When their dad had taken the twins to their Gran's and Gramps's to live, he'd said to Hardy Flower, 'Here you are, son – this is for you.'

In his hand Mr Hardy Thomas held a bent machine-gun bullet which a German pilot had fired at the factory where he worked; it had still been hot when he had picked it up. The small missile became Hardy Flower's most prized possession, which he kept in his waistcoat pocket, only to be worn on Sundays. Very often, Hardy Flower showed the bullet to the village kids to stop them having a go at Daisy and himself. The twins were the outsiders and they weren't allowed to forget it.

Very often the twins sat on a wall watching the mums and dads take their kids to the village pub for lemonade and crisps. Hardy Flower and Daisy were loners and treated like foreigners with their 'sarf-east' accents.

Early one Sunday morning their Gran whispered to the twins: 'Make haste home from Sunday schoo'el, moi dearrs, as you'm mum an' dad ull be 'eer when you'm get back.'

Off to Sunday school they went, Daisy in her best dress and Hardy Flower in his best Sunday suit. For some unknown reason, that Sunday didn't get off to a very good start for the twins because the village kids had been pushing and shoving them around and nit-picking at them. The weather was very wet, and Hardy Flower had fallen over in a cow pat and smothered his best suit in best-quality cow dung. As they walked along the mile-long lane towards their Gran's cottage, Hardy Flower became very upset at what they would all think when he and Daisy arrived home. 'They' being Gran and Gramps, their Uncle Tom and, of course, their parents, whom they hadn't seen for several months. The Battle of Britain was at its height.

Hardy Flower felt ill with a stomach ache and, more than anything, he felt very frightened. Then, unfortunately and very suddenly, he messed himself and stood there petrified as he continually vacated his bowels. The overpowering smell was unbelievable, as was the pain raging inside his stomach. Daisy stood there crying her eyes out. Neither of them knew what to do in that long, lonely lane. And, what would his dad say when he found out that Hardy Flower didn't have

31

that bullet? His Uncle Tom had taken Hardy Flower's bullet to the village pub, to boast about in front of the other cowhands. It had got him a free pint from the landlord, and Hardy Flower had not yet got that bullet back from his Uncle Tom. (He never would.)

Daisy and her brother walked slowly along the wet country lane, picking at tufts of grass to clean Hardy Flower off with. Of course, the village kids suddenly appeared and thought it was great fun to plague them with their cat-calls.

'You'm a dirty foreign kid.'

'Ee'm messed his trouwserrrs.'

'Do 'ee want 'is mummy 'en?'

'Shitty-legs! Shitty-legs!'

'Ooh argh! Worse'n 'a cows an' pigs, 'ee be!'

'We'm clean kids we'm be, un us? Let's push 'em both in 'a pond an' run away?'

The other kids just laughed and ran off.

And 'shitty-legs' Hardy Flower was, looking as if he had walked through a cow field up to his thighs. The catcalls continued all the way along the lane to the village where the children went their own way. Daisy and Hardy Flower were a sorry sight when they finally reached their Gran's house where their parents greeted them with a kiss – a welcome cuddle had to wait, under the circumstances.

Uncle Tom, whom the twins both loved, smiled and spoke in his Gloucestershire accent:

'Ooh-arrgh! Oi doo belaeve the boy 'as shat 'issalf.'

Sometime during the twins' stay with their Gran, they had to have a medical examination at the village school, where it was discovered that both Daisy and Hardy Flower had caught impetigo. At that time it was considered to be caused by not washing and bad hygiene. The school headmaster, Mr Bullock, was heard to say: 'Dirty little swine! I thought they'd know better, coming from London way.'

At that, the twins' elder sister Rose went berserk and,

despite her twelve years, she went for the headmaster and put him in his place. It was the first time the teacher had ever been pulled into line by a young schoolgirl. Rose had always stood by Daisy and Hardy Flower, but, being older, she sometimes needed and sought the friendship of older girls, going to their houses after school and at the weekends, making the twins vulnerable to the youngest of the village bullies.

The treatment for impetigo in that time of ignorance was the continual application of neat peroxide, which caused the infected area to sizzle and burn, much to the twins' discomfort. Once the infected area was burnt and crusted over, it was then considered that there was no need to worry about further infection.

The village school had two classrooms with a dividing wall, which was a folding partition. This stopped the air flowing through and always made Hardy Flower feel sleepy. There was one occasion during lunch break, when the seven-year-old boy became very much wide awake. His sandwiches were spread with a very insipid-looking meat paste which always made him 'gag' and feel quite sick. When the lunch break started, a little girl of his own age whispered to him: 'If you'm give Oi a paste sandwich, Oi'll show you moine – if you show me your'n?'

Naturally, Hardy Flower was all in favour of doing a swap, so he handed her one of his paste sandwiches, hoping to be handed something in return. Much to his surprise, however, there was no sandwich being offered. Instead, up went the little girl's skirt as her legs parted, then, lo and behold, there in front of Hardy Flower's eyes was a puffed-up 'V', tiny, red and bare, being held wide open with two small and grubby index fingers. It was his very first lesson in human biology.

As Hardy Flower handed over his fourth and last sandwich, in payment for the fourth and final biology lesson, he felt a sudden and violent smack hard across his ear. He and his fellow biology student were very rapidly whisked apart by the scruff of their collars. It was the first time Hardy Flower had ever heard the oath, 'Oh my God!' Miss Dance, the teacher, was there, almost fainting in shock at what she had come across in the infants' classroom, and from then onwards the little country maiden and Hardy Flower were always kept apart.

Hardy Flower could never understand why. After all, the little girl had told him: 'If moi mam can show moi dad 'er's out in tha' woodshed – if moi dad showed 'err 'is, whoi couldn't Oi show moine at schoo'el?'

Hardy Flower didn't mind the 'going' to school, because there were lots of things down the lane to hold his interest, all day and every day. Once he and Daisy had crossed over the old Bristol Road, they could either climb over a wooden stile and go over the fields, or they could go to the crossroads and turn left at the old village police station. If they climbed over the stile, the first thing they had to watch out for was an enormous white bull. That big old bull didn't wait for a red flag to be waved, he just charged. When the twins reached the other side of the field they went into an apple or pear orchard, on the other side of which was a cow field. The cows always wandered over to them, to see whether they had anything for them to eat, like an apple, but their size always frightened the twins, so they didn't hang about. Another stile took them into the lane which led them to school. All the hedgerows were kept trimmed neat and tidy by the farm labourers, who whistled and sang as they used their billhooks expertly.

Sometimes Daisy and Hardy Flower ran up to the crossroads where there was a clump of apple trees near the village duck pond, to look for windfalls. One particular tree stood at the edge of the police station garden, and the village policeman didn't like children, especially those who didn't belong to the village and especially if they were after his apples. The police station was no bigger than an ordinary house and the duck pond seemed so deep, still and mysterious.

After nicking the windfalls the twins turned into 'The Lane' as the villagers called it. Like all lanes, this one was not straight. At each bend there was something else to look at – they never knew what was going to happen round the corner. Sometimes they would go running down the lane and come across a herd of cows going back to the fields, after having had their early-morning milking. Further on, they would see a massive great farm waggon being pulled by two magnificent shire horses. Very often the twins made themselves late for school because they had ridden part of the way on top of the hay waggon, sneaking a crafty ride. It was so easy to fall asleep among the hay or straw, especially if the sun was shining.

Down The Lane lived the local doctor and further down lived the parson, and both of them always glared at Hardy Flower, especially when he tried to give them his friendliest smile. Both of their gardeners were friendly to Daisy and Hardy Flower, except when the 'master' or the 'mistress' were 'at home'.

The posh and more privileged kids also lived down The Lane and they went into Gloucester to their 'paid for' schools. They wore long socks with coloured patterns interwoven in the turnover tops below their knees and matching school belts with a silver 'snake' clasp at the waist. To Hardy Flower, all posh kids seemed to have sticky-out ears to support their oversize school caps. Every day the posh kids caught the school bus into the city, and of course Hardy Flower thought they were all little mummy's pets, all jockeying for favour and to be the school sneak. How he envied all the opportunities which he thought they had!

Down The Lane the twins often saw lots of tramps and vagrants – the dropouts and down-and-outers. They were filthy dirty and wore two or three pairs of trousers, with large bundles of pots and pans hanging from the string which was tied round their waist. The tramps and vagrants all wore beards and were of an eccentric nature. The kids called and jeered after them, and then the be-whiskered dropouts would shout back, shaking their fists and waving their sticks and staves, scaring the living daylights out of them. It was thought that some of the tramps were German spies or conscientious objectors – according to the grown-up and small-minded gossips in the village.

A very familiar sight along the old Bristol road for any children was the low-loaders, the lorries which transported the parts of crashed or shot-down aircraft back to a factory for repairs or replacements. That was about the nearest the villages ever got to the war as farmers and farmhands were exempt from war service.

There was only one tiny general store in the village, and that was attached to the side of a very small garage. It was there that Hardy Flower had to take the huge glass acid accumulator batteries to be charged.

The twins, Gran and Gramps, with their Uncle Tom, always sat round the accumulator radio set, then Gran would say: 'Hark. Let's listen to the news, to see how the war is going.'

'Hark' was one of Gran's favourite words. After the news, which was all that the family ever listened to, she would thrill her three grandchildren by telling them tales of 'Jack the Ripper', events which she thought she could just about remember.

Their Gran's stories half frightened them to death as they sat in the spooky old cottage at night-time. As she terrorised them with her old stories, the flame of the paraffin lamp would flicker, making all the shadows dance up and down on the walls. None of the kids dared move, their teeth chattering as their eyes grew wide with horror. Their old Gran would cackle into her jug of stout and then send them to bed.

As there was no electricity in the village, they had to go up the rickety old stairs with a flickering candle to light their way, the shadows at their side moving in all directions as they went up each stair. There were no carpets, mats or lino on the floors in their gran's old cottage, which meant that each floorboard creaked and groaned as they stepped on it. Even in bed, they would hold each other's hands until they went to sleep.

Their gran didn't have either gas or fresh water laid on, and all the cooking was done over a huge fireplace which lay between two huge cast-iron ovens. All her cooking utensils were made of cast iron, and when they were used, they were hooked on to a swinging chain which disappeared up the chimney. A small barrel-shaped saucepan and a huge frying pan were always on top of the ovens. Everything was pushed, pulled, or tipped when the utensil hung on the hook over the fire.

Drinking water was carried from a freshwater spring which was situated at the bottom of the hill on which Gran lived. The spring always seemed so dark and mysterious because it was surrounded by slabs of rock weed and bracken. They were warned: 'If you'm goes too near to that therr're spring, they'm mermaids 'ull leap up and git yees.' Close by was a watercress bed which Hardy Flower liked to wade through to pick and eat the cress. The canal, which had a hump-backed bridge over it, also had locks on either side for the bargees to operate, and the overspill of water filled up a large duck pond, where the kids played, chasing the ducks and looking for the ducks' eggs.

Fresh water had to be carried the six hundred yards up the hill to the cottage. It was a long way to carry two two-gallon buckets filled with water, but to make the carrying easier the buckets were hooked on to a carved wooden yoke which fitted across the shoulders and round the neck. To stop the water splashing over the rims of the buckets as they swayed, a twig was floated on the surface of the water to check slopping about. Hardy Flower didn't use the yoke or the big buckets until he was twelve years old and then he would carry only the one-gallon buckets for his gran.

4

Life Gets Rougher.
The Battle of Britain Continues

Life was primitive in the village of Whitminster during the wartime days, but then life hadn't been luxurious or even comfortable back at home either.

One of the uncomfortable things that everybody experienced in the village was not being able to use a flushing lavatory. As there was no running water, anybody who needed to answer the calls of nature had to walk up to the end of their garden and enter the 'thunder box', a small wooden establishment that served as the toilet. Most lavatories in the countryside consisted of a wooden seat, with two holes, and underneath each hole a rather large oval bucket. The shed in the garden was variously known as 'the throne room', 'the karsi', 'a place to rest', or 'the bog'. Hardy Flower's gran used all of those expressions, depending on her mood, or her particular need at the time. Unfortunately, for some, those buckets were emptied only when it was absolutely necessary, into a large hole which had been dug especially for that purpose.

The first obstacles for Hardy Flower, Daisy and Rose when visiting the 'thunder box' were three very deep stone steps outside the back door. Anybody climbing them would have to most certainly use the very old and rickety wooden railing, to assist their climb upwards. The second obstacle was the rough flint pathway which led upwards to the chicken coop and the 'double-seated throne room', which were adjoining. Sometimes, the twins were told, old Gramps would sometimes just make it to the chicken coop, and on other occasions eggs were found in the 'thunder box'.

It was even more uncomfortable in the middle of the night, especially in the winter when the children had to creep up to that place of rest and try not to disturb the hens. The grown-ups shared a bucket, which was kept at the top of the stairs. As unpleasant as it sounds, it was customary to take a dock leaf or a handful of soft grass while on a visit to the 'throne of contentment'. That was in the summer – perhaps, in the winter, it was a handful of snow! Naturally, the country gardens always had the best vegetable plots the children had ever seen.

Gran and Gramps were both lovely old people, and there were memorable things they both did which Daisy and Hardy Flower would never forget. Gramps always had a huge cup and saucer, which held a pint of tea. There were no such things as tea bags in those far-off days, tea was made from loose tea leaves. The measure was one teaspoon of leaves per person, and one for the pot. Gran and Gramps never used a tea-strainer. When Gramps had a cup of tea, his habit was to fill his saucer with tea, saying it would cool his tea quicker. When the old man slurped his tea the saucer was balanced on the tips of his fingers, on one or both hands.

When he drank the customary way, straight from the cup, it went in one gulp, but the tea leaves were left on Gramps' teeth. Then, using his lips, he would expertly deposit the tea leaves back on the inside rim of the teacup. Gramps never wasted those tea leaves. After the second cup of tea, he mixed them together with two heaped teaspoons of sugar, making what he called his 'slops', which was his roughage. He always invited Daisy and Hardy Flower to share it. Afterwards, he'd grab Daisy and bounce her on his knee, whispering in his

deep shire accent in her ear: 'Daisy Anne Maroi'arr! – Piddled
… in the foi're!' This mildly obscene outburst always had
the twins in stitches.

Gramps was a farm labourer and cowhand all his working
life, which meant he started work in the early hours of the
morning. Three times a day he went home for his meals, and
after he had finished the evening milking he and all the local
farm workers met in the village pub, where they stayed until
they felt ready for bed, though at that time pubs were always
closed up by ten o'clock.

Gran was the mother of seven children, two boys and five
girls, and she was a cripple, having been a victim of poliomyelitis
when she was a young girl. Gran's hair was a silvery-grey
and very curly; she looked the Romany type, which was
prevalent in her family. Gran only had one tooth, at the top
front, and she would always boast to the twins: 'That's moi
pickled on'yun too'th. Oi sticks an on'yun on 'im to suck,
because sweets are bad for moiy too'thy pegs!'

When Granny Thomas was happy and in a good mood,
she'd whistle loud and melodious, her favourite tune being
'If I was a Blackbird'. When she whistled, it was the sound
of a blackbird, warbling and trilling, which always made the
twins feel happy.

Although their Gran was also crippled with arthritis, she still
had to carry water from the spring, putting on a big black
taffeta hat, and sticking a great big hat pin through it, saying,
'A lady never gaws out without her hat.' Then she would limp
down to the spring in her long ankle-length black dress and
then limp back with two backbreaking buckets of water. It
took her a morning, or an afternoon, to make the return trip.
'It's a walk out in the fresh air, and it will do moi leg good,'
she would say. The spring water was only for cooking and
drinking. For any other use, she used the rainwater, which she
saved in the huge water barrels outside the back door.

During the summer evenings Granny Thomas would limp

41

up the hill to the village inn, carrying a large jug, and go into The Jug and Bottle where she would buy a jugful of 'Special Stout'. Then, having taken a hefty swig, she would limp back to her cottage and sit on the wall, drinking her stout, and eating bread and cheese for her supper. Sometimes, Hardy Flower would have a taste of both, which he found quite delicious. The stout always made him tired and ready for bed, especially when he could hear the birds singing and the droning hum of the bees.

Very often, the twins' cousin Ray cycled out to Whitminster for the day. At that time, the two boys were inseparable, going everywhere together. They made bows and arrows and held contests with other kids, who became friendlier when their cousin Ray was with them. Ray and Hardy Flower liked to go fishing with the fishing rods which they made themselves, or sometimes they went swimming, or they stayed at home with their gran and her old dog. Sometimes they played in their secret camp under the hedge overhanging a chicken run. Only their gran was allowed to know where it was and to know their secret sign and special password. When the two boys were together, Daisy usually tagged along at a distance, always ready to do their bidding. Sometimes they asked her to stand watch.

One sunny afternoon, Hardy Flower and Ray heard Daisy's warning whistle, which made the two heroes become very furtive. In unison, they looked out straight at the knees of a posh-looking lady and gentleman who stood looking down at their grubby faces. The two boys peered round the legs and through the branches and saw a young lad of their own age, seven or eight. The two suspicious cousins looked at the 'posh kid' who was wearing a toy soldier's uniform and cap, all made to measure. The posh kid also carried a toy pop-gun, which fired a cork attached to a string on the barrel. From above, and still peering down into their camp, were the two upside-down faces. Then the two cousins heard:

'These two boys, Ian, are your cousins!' neighed the posh lady. Then, to Ray and Hardy Flower, she snapped: 'Play with your cousin Ian, nicely, you two!'

The 'posh lady' and her husband then walked into the cottage to see Gran.

The 'lady' peering through her pince-nez was the better-off sister of Hardy Flower's father, and also the sister of Ray's mother. The two boys had heard of their 'posh aunt' whose name was Gwendoline. She had done well for herself up in 'Ber'ming'gam' and had married a 'rich man'.

The two boys' cousin, Ian, they found out, was an only child, and at that moment probably felt quite alone as Ray and Hardy Flower slowly and slyly 'interrogated' him. Ian was one of those 'posh kids', at least by their standards. For instance, Ray's and Hardy Flower's weekly 'bath' was in the canal – they had one every day if the weather was warm. But it was well known that Aunt Gwendoline had a bathroom! However, Ian was lonely and wanted to play with his two newly found cousins.

The two cousins compromised: he could play with them if Hardy Flower had Ian's rifle and Ray wore his tailor-made soldier's tunic. Ray, like Hardy Flower, was long and lanky, so that when he put the uniform jacket on the sleeves came almost up to his elbows. The toy rifle looked like a pea-shooter on a string over Hardy Flower's shoulder.

However, Ian was only too pleased to be able to share his toys with his nice but rough cousins. The three cousins even allowed Daisy to participate as a lady spy, or, in the second battle, as an Indian squaw, to fetch and carry. To Ian's delight, it was Ian, Ray and Hardy Flower, with Daisy tailing behind, versus the Jones kids, who lived next door. And so, because Hardy Flower 'actually' came from where they 'actually' had bombs dropped on people, he was the sergeant and in charge, so that eventually he and his two commandos won the war. The Jones boys had been the Germans. In the second battle, the three cousins, as Indians with their squaw Daisy, had also beaten the cowboys.

Hot and sweaty, they lolled about as they threw grass seed 'arrows' at the chickens and ducks, making the waterfowl scoot away hurriedly. In the warm afternoon sunshine they planned another war game – to the three cousins' advantage, of course.

Suddenly, the real enemy came in sight, holding her head high, and peering down at them again through her pince-nez, her disdainfully raised eyebrows, and puckered lips, suggested that something didn't smell quite right. Sniff-sniff! In an affected voice, she tra-la'd: 'Come along, Ian! We have a bus to catch!' Even they didn't have a car in those days.

Very wistfully, and most reluctantly, Hardy Flower gave Ian his gun back, and Ray handed back the now torn and very soiled tunic. Much to their surprise, Aunt Gwendoline handed Ray, Daisy and Hardy Flower a halfpenny each. Like long-lost friends, Ray and Hardy Flower went to the bus-stop to see Ian off back to the city, with all of them making plans for the next time they met. The three country cousins had enjoyed their newly found city cousin's company.

Hardy Flower only ever saw his cousin Ian once more, when once again he appeared with his mother on a quick visit to see his mother's brother, Uncle Thomas. Unfortunately, Ian had grown up to be a very effeminate alcoholic, who minced along the road with his limp wrist held high while holding the leash of a white miniature poodle. Protruding from his hip pocket was the neck of a whisky flask. Within five years, he had fallen, while in a drunken stupor, on to an electric fire, resulting in a most unpleasant death.

As the three cousins never had any pocket money, Aunt Gwendoline's halfpenny was a fortune to them. There were no sweet shops in the village, so Daisy, Ray and Hardy Flower, asked their Gran if there was anywhere that they could buy some sweets for a halfpenny. In her West-Country accent she advised them: 'Well, moi deerrs, if you'm could wait a few days, the little house up the Bristol roa'd is the village post office, and they'm hoping to get some chocolate bars in, and they'm moight just let you'm have some on'it.'

In between their gran's cottage and the post office house was a huge old house in which two old spinster sisters lived, the Misses Shepherd, and about one hundred yards further up the Bristol road was the post office. Although it was only a small house, they identified it by the small Victorian mailbox set into the wall outside the front door.

The house consisted of the front room downstairs, which was the post office, separated from the hallway by a stable door. The bottom half, when the shop was open, was the counter. Hardy Flower and Ray could just about reach the top of the counter with their fingers, pulling themselves up so that their eyes were just level to see over the top. The proprietor didn't like children and was always suspicious of them. The chocolate bars which he sold were not part of his proper store; somehow or other he obtained the chocolate bars from the nearby Cadbury's factory – no doubt on the black market. It was rumoured that he doubled his prices for children because no adults would buy the chocolate from him.

After their cousin Ray returned home to the city, the twins were once again on their own. The Jones boys next door didn't really have time for the twins and they gradually built up a kind of hatred for 'they'm from Lunnon way'.

Miss Matilda and Miss Annie Shepherd, the ex-teacher spinster sisters, didn't like Hardy Flower one bit. One of the sisters had called out to him while he was swinging on their squeaking iron front gate: 'Get off of that gate, you horrid boy, and stop picking your nose! Oh, you horrible nosy little brat! I'll have a word with your Grandma-ma about you. Go away at once, you disgusting creature!'

The other neighbours, the Joneses, lived in the former servants' quarters of Hill-View, so Mrs Wire was considered to be the real neighbour. She was different from Matilda and Annie Shepherd. Mrs Wire was a kindly old soul who took to Hardy Flower and his twin sister. The kind old lady kept lots of chickens. She sold the fresh eggs in the village and fattened the hens up for her customers' Christmas dinners. One day one of her chickens spread its wings and escaped. Having flown its coop, it landed and strutted through the hedge into Hardy Flower's 'jungle' beyond, where it clucked its way forward hungrily, looking for food. Quite unsuspecting, the handsome Rhode Island Red was followed by a ferocious 'jungle cat', a huge striped beast of a tomcat named Tiger, the darling pet of Annie and Matilda.

As Tiger stalked the mother hen, Hardy Flower stalked Tiger. Unfortunately, the jungle into which they had all crept was the garden of Miss Annie and Miss Matilda Shepherd.

Crouched down in the shade of the redcurrent bushes, Hardy Flower raised his bow and aimed an arrow at the tiger. Hardy Flower was Robin Hood, the famous archer, and Robin Hood could never miss that tiger, or so he thought. Zing-zing-zing – his arrows were falling all around the suddenly frightened moggie.

'Three more arrows should do it!' thought Hardy Flower, not thinking for one second what he would do if he trapped or injured the 'tiger'.

Suddenly the neck of his jersey tightened, and Hardy Flower was lifted up off his feet. Then his ear started to burn from the blow of Miss Matilda Shepherd's ham-like right hand. 'You horrible little beast!' she screamed. 'You detestable boy!'

Hardy Flower felt a warm loosening sensation somewhere in the seat of his pants, and he sincerely hoped that he hadn't done what he thought he had done when he last wore his best Sunday suit.

Miss Matilda Shepherd continued with her tirade, hissing the word 'boy' as if it was an incurable disease.

'How dare you, boy, fire your arrows at my poor little tabby-kins!' she shouted as she shook the living daylight out of Hardy Flower.

Finally she lowered him to the ground and, as his feet touched the earth, she gave Hardy Flower such a shove that he found himself back through the hole in the hedge. No bow and no arrows. It was then that Hardy Flower decided that he would have to kill Miss Matilda Shepherd.

Hardy Flower made another bow and lots of arrows, whose tips he dipped into the juice of crushed deadly nightshade berries. His Gran had told him that the berries were a deadly poison. Then every day Hardy Flower fired his arrows over the hedge, and just in case he and his fat spinster foe met face to face, he carried one of his gran's broken dinner knives stuck into his belt so he could stab her.

Hardy Flower never did see either of the two sisters again. In his mind, he imagined that he must have killed them with his bow and arrows. And, for months and months, until he returned home to Kent, he expected to be arrested every time he saw the village policeman.

The countryside was losing its lovely autumn colours and the nights were getting darker and colder. One night, Daisy, Rose and Hardy Flower sat near the kitchen stove, having a last warm before they went to bed, when suddenly there was the ringing of an ambulance bell, as it rushed past the cottage. In those days the emergency bell was perched on top of the ambulance, and was rung using a rope inside. At that time of night the only sound they would usually hear was the sound of nature settling down for the night, creatures hunting, or the wind and rain. Occasionally, the sound of a motor vehicle would come and go within seconds. When an ambulance went by, with its bell ringing, their Gran would sing one of her ditties.

Harrk! Harrk! The dogs do barrk!
The beggarrs ar're coming to town!
Some's in rags, and some's in bags,
And some's in velvet gowns!

In the village and all around, the farmers and cowhands wondered where the ambulance was going along that quiet and dark lonely road, late at night. However, off to bed they went, and very soon Rose was telling them a story in her spookiest voice:

The dark, dark, man!
Went up a dark, dark, street!
On a dark, dark, night!
Then, he went up a dark, dark, alley!
And he went up a dark, dark, path!
Then, he went into a dark, dark, house!
And he went up some dark, dark, stairs...

The twins were lying cuddled up to Rose, absolutely petrified. Their eyes rolled round in their sockets, looking for the slightest movement in the flickering shadows thrown by the single candle, listening for the slightest sound. In her deepest voice, Rose continued:

Then he went into a dark, dark, room!
And then a dark, dark voice shouted, 'HOI!-YOI!-YOU!!'

Rose went into peals of laughter, as Daisy and Hardy Flower both jumped out of their skins and dived underneath the blankets.

When they got up the next morning, Gran told the children that their Uncle Tom had heard that a lorry had hit the bridge over the canal, near the freshwater spring and somersaulted into the canal, where the driver had drowned.

The ambulance had arrived too late to save his life. It was a rare occurrence to see an ambulance come out from the city. Afterwards it was the topic of conversation in the village for many weeks, especially after Uncle Tom showed the locals a pile of pennies which had fallen straight from the driver's pocket. Perhaps their quick-thinking Uncle Tom used his own coins as 'props' as a way of encouraging the country yokels to listen to his story.

Suddenly the weather became very cold. It was now December and with it came a lot of snow. Daisy and Hardy Flower went down to the duck pond, knowing that it was frozen over. Hardy Flower decided that he would skate on it. When they got there, there was nobody else on it, which meant it was all his!

'Cor! Watch me slide right across the duck pond!'

Long and skinny, the boy took a long run down the bank, and took off across the ice. It was a terrific feeling to balance and sway, to waver and slide, until, suddenly, there was on almighty ker'rack as the ice splintered all round the now very lonely and frightened boy. Hardy Flower was in the pond, up to his armpits in the freezing water, which promptly soaked through his short trousers and flimsy jersey.

Daisy clambered to the edge of the cracked and broken ice and supported Hardy Flower under his armpits Both of the twins were frightened out of their young wits, but there was not a tear in sight.

Fortunately there was a farmhand's cottage near the duck pond, and within minutes a hefty lad managed to drag the half-frozen children to safety. Hardy Flower was feeling very sorry for himself, standing there with his teeth chattering, while the water from the duck pond dripped from his sodden clothes and his bare hands and knees turned a bright red. With his teeth chattering like a frozen woodpecker's beak, Hardy Flower and Daisy walked up the frozen and snow-packed hill to their Gran's cottage, soaked through and freezing.

At that time, the eldest sister Rose and her ageing gran had started to have words. The situation had got to a point where Hardy Flower thought that the three of them were getting on Gran's nerves. She and Gramps were getting very crotchety. The novelty of Gran and Gramps having them there had worn off. So, when Hardy Flower came out of that pond, he knew that Gran wouldn't be very pleased.

The twins took their time, hoping to dry off before they saw their sister Rose and their Gran. They sneaked in, trying not to disturb her 'catnap', but Gran woke up instantly and saw the state that Hardy Flower was in. Hardy Flower fully expected her to get very angry, but she spoke kindly.

'Ooh'arrh! You'm a pair o' poor little moites! What happened, for you'm to be into that state? Oi dawn't knaw!'

If she hadn't said anything, Hardy Flower could have just gone in and put his Sunday best suit trousers on, and hidden the wet ones until they were dry. Hardy Flower stood there on the bare flagstones shivering with cold, his teeth still chattering, and his knees knocking together. He was afraid to cry, in case his Gran got angry with them. But the old lady showed the twins a lot of sympathy and compassion. However, Hardy Flower was ready to cry, and when his Granny took his hand and led him to the kitchen fire with a washed-out oatmeal sack wrapped round his waist, he let himself go and cried his eyes out. Within seconds Daisy joined her twin and they shed their tears together, sometimes in unison, and sometimes in descant like an alley-cats' choir.

In the back of the house there was a scullery, which could have been a kitchen, but all there was in it was a shallow tub, with no water taps, to do the laundry in; their Gran used rainwater. The root vegetables from the garden were also stored there in boxes. Quite often, the chickens came in to peck about and sort out the creepy-crawlies. The horse's harness hung there, giving off a strong smell of horse sweat and leather. Against the wall, leading to the living room-cum-kitchen, were stacked the wooden logs which Uncle Tom had split with an axe. It was Hardy Flower's job to carry the logs into the house. In another corner stood a scythe and two pitchforks for haymaking. In the old dark cupboards under the stairs, cats had kittens and played with the mice.

At Christmas time, the chickens had their necks stretched; they were the seasonal Christmas dinner in those days, and that was where Hardy Flower learned to pluck chickens. The feathers seemed to float about for ever. It was all part of country life.

Rose took Daisy and Hardy Flower into Gloucester, just before Christmas, to deliver the chickens for their Auntie Gwendoline's Christmas dinner. There was a lot of snow still carpeting everywhere. The bus always stopped outside the village police station, and when the weather was fine, the bus came along three times a day, but in snowy weather they were very often held up.

Once in the city, it was a treat for all three children to look into the shop windows, and while they did so, a sailor spoke to Rose. There was no fear of strangers during the wartime years.

'Where do you come from then, miss?'

When Rose answered him, he exclaimed, 'I know that accent! I come from that way myself!'

He then gave the three waif-like children four threepenny pieces and said, 'Have a happy Christmas, kids!'

Those threepenny pieces seemed like a fortune to the children then.

The Whitminster schoolchildren always had a Christmas party every year, in the village hall, and although there was a war on, it didn't deter the Christmas spirit. The village hall was decorated with the coloured paper-chains, which the children had made up at school, then once the balloons were up, too, the atmosphere became quite seasonal. There was a nice carpet of snow, and everybody was getting ready for

Christmas Day. On the day of the children's party, everyone talked about it all day at school, and everybody was happy and excited. During the evening all the kids and the two or three teachers would enjoy the party, and then break up for the Christmas period.

Home they all went, Hardy Flower, Daisy and Rose, to get ready for the party. They had a quick 'lick and a spit' wash, in front of Gran's fire, then Daisy and Rose put on their best dress, while Hardy Flower wore his Sunday best suit. They put on their wellies and macs and off they went to the party.

The three children became very excited as they trudged through the snow up the hill, and when they got to the crossroads they could see the shaded lights and decorations of the village hall, which made them even more excited, and as they approached the police station duck pond Hardy Flower could see the reflections of the coloured lights flickering on the water. 'What a lovely Christmas feeling,' he thought to himself.

All they had to do then was cross the road, go into the hall, change their wellies for their slippers and enjoy the party. But when they got to the door and stood craning their heads and necks to see what was going on they could see Rose talking to somebody. That somebody growled:

'You'm b'aint a'comin' in yere, you Thomases! You'm bain't o' the village, you'm kids bain't, un' this 'yere is a Christmas parrrty forr the village chillun only!'

The village hall caretaker was in his element as he stood with his clenched fists on his fat hips. On his feet he still wore his manure boots. Rose, Daisy and Hardy Flower just stood there, Hardy Flower holding his cap in hand, trying to show his manners. They couldn't understand why they were not allowed into the hall with the other school kids. The twins tried to peer round the fat belly of the red-faced caretaker, but all they could see was the huge brass buckle of his heavy leather belt holding up his dung-stained and smelly corduroys.

So that they didn't miss out on everything, they hung outside the village hall, standing in the slush and snow like three begging waifs, listening to the fun and games of the village children's Christmas party.

After a few games had been played, somebody came out. Obviously the three evacuees thought they were being invited in, but all they heard was: 'You'm Thomas kids better be off! You'm get yum'selfs away to wher' youm's belong! Youm's Lunnoners no roight to be yere, be you'm gone afore we'm cawll the police'n!'

The three rejected and dejected evacuees dragged themselves back through the snow again, back to their Gran's house. None of them cried; they just accepted what they had been told – 'Get yourselves home!' It just made them miss their mum and dad just that bit more. 'Home' for the three Thomas kids was a long, long, way away in 1940.

Most of the village kids came and gloatingly showed them the Christmas presents they had received. There were penknives, paint sets, dolls, books, sets of this and sets of that, and some kids were fortunate enough to have been given two gifts, because there were some to spare, and because their mums had helped out with the party.

But the more fortunate children, as innocent as they were, had no idea how much it had hurt Hardy Flower and his sisters. And to think that Hardy Flower had smarmed his hair down and dressed up, smarter than the school sneak, only to be 'sent on his way'!

The Thomas children's Christmas that year was an extra piece of chicken for dinner, and they were allowed to stay up a bit later than usual and have a sip of their Gran's Stout and a smell of Gramp's and Uncle Tom's whisky. On Boxing Day the landed gentry gathered at Whitminster Inn, for the usual fox hunt. The fox hunters, all fat and purple-nosed from their abundant tippling, looked more like 'hunters', than the horses themselves.

While the locals lackeyed, and touched their forelocks, the 'upper crust' of the Berkley Hunt chased the fox through the snow-blanketed countryside. Finally brought to bay, it lay panting and out of breath. Then, without any mercy, the hounds tore it to pieces. At the end of the hunt, the 'novice hunters' paraded themselves at the village inn, splashes of the fox's blood daubed on their brave faces! There were cries of 'Drinks all round, if you please, Landlord!'

After Christmas, while they were still off school, Hardy Flower, with his sisters Daisy and Rose, played out in the snowy fields. On their return to the cottage, Gran asked, 'Where's your glove, Daisy?' Daisy was wearing only one. Of course, this meant that straight away they had to return to the fields and woods to find that lost glove.

Back out into the snow they went, charging in and out of the snow drifts, having the time of their life at the same time, but knowing all the same that they daren't go back without Daisy's lost glove. Eventually, the children found it lying in the middle of a field, where they had churned up the snow. Luckily, they just saw a fingertip of the glove sticking though the snow.

Back inside the cottage, the children did their best to dry their clothes, but because they had to wear them until bedtime, they were still wet the next morning when they went outside again.

Gran's love and attention seemed to be diminishing as the weeks went by, and as much as she loved her three grandchildren her attitude had changed; she just didn't show the same interest in them any more. Granny Evelyn Thomas was an old and tired lady, with very little patience left. The growing and boisterous children were gradually wearing her down and playing on her nerves.

Suddenly, one weekend, their father Hardy Thomas arrived,

to stay for a few days, telling them that they were all going home. Of course, the children were overjoyed at the news.

There was no fuss and bother, either when they left Gran, Gramps and Uncle Tom, or when they arrived home. They gave their mum just a quick 'Hello' and then they went straight out into the garden to play. There wasn't much to stay indoors for and Mrs Flower Thomas was busy, running backwards and forwards, taking care of an old man who was on the verge of dying.

Mrs Flower Thomas was not at all fond of housework, or cleaning, or cooking. Mrs Flower Thomas always stated that her vocation was nursing. It was very often that she sat with somebody who was very ill, and when the patient eventually died, she was there to 'lay them out'. To Mrs Flower Thomas, it was nothing to wash the body and prepare it for the coffin, ready for family and friends when they came in to view and pay their last respects.

Once, on her return from such a 'laying out', her son Hardy Flower overheard her remark to her husband:

'That was a difficult one, Hardy! His family have been away, and while they were away, the old granddad "pegged out" and the rigor mortis had set in. I had to sit on his knees to straighten them, and then I had to crack and force the shoulder joint, to get his arm in the coffin. I don't want too many like that!'

Another time Hardy Flower went with his mum to a neighbour's house, where an old man was laid on the table waiting for his coffin to be delivered. He had not yet been laid out. This was plain enough even for Hardy Flower to see, as the boy watched with grim fascination, his chin resting on the edge of the table top.

Rigor mortis had set in, raising the corpse's buttocks several inches above the table. The skinny old boy wasn't wearing any sort of burial suit, only a thread-bare long-sleeved woollen vest through which the curve of his ribs showed. At the tattered and buttonless 'V' at the neck, a few sparse white hairs sprouted. About his nether regions, he wore a pair of well-worn, sagging long-johns, which displayed another bunch of white tufted hair surrounding a very dead manhood. Underneath his bony hips, sagging down to the table top and weighted down with natural body waste, was his button-up 'shitter-flap', stained and unwashed. Then, as if his dear old wife was doing him a favour while she showed him off, the old lady had tried to poke a very bony big toe back through a strangulating hole in a well-darned sock.

With his eyes popping and his mouth open, Hardy Flower was dragged by his grimy ears away from the parlour table, past the sagging mouth with its hastily inserted ill-fitting dentures. To the awe-stricken boy, it seemed as if the dead glassy eyes were staring sideways at him from their slowly opening eyelids. Hardy Flower had seen his first dead body and the memory would stay with him for ever.

5

1941, Home Again and The Battle of Britain's Finished

The twins were now at Cecil Road Junior School, which was very different from going to the village school at Whitminster where Hardy Flower and Daisy had been well and truly on their own. There had not been many children at the village school, but there had been enough to make their school days there very uncomfortable. But, at home, when they went back to the junior school they still had problems, especially when they were referred to as 'those kids, who talk funny'. The twins had picked up the Gloucestershire accent and their home-town accent seemed strange to them.

Life was just as easy-going and just as rough. By that time, their brother Clifford was in the army; the two other brothers, Ken and Jim, were not yet old enough, but their time would come eventually. Hardy Flower was highly delighted when his hero brother Clifford came home on weekend leave. Clifford was fully kitted up with all his army equipment, complete with his rifle, bayonet and a magazine loaded with live bullets. For their soldier son's short stay, his weapons of war were put in Mr and Mrs Thomas's bedroom for safety. Because nobody was allowed into this sanctum under any circumstances, the weapons and ammunition were considered to be 'out of harm's way and in a safe place'.

Everybody had gone out, leaving Hardy Flower alone in

the house, and being of an inquisitive nature, or, to put it more bluntly, 'a nosy little bugger', the adventurous young boy decided that it would be good for him to be able to play with a real gun and 'sword'. He knew that the 'sword' fitted on to the end of the .303 rifle. Up the bare and dusty stairs he ran, full of his own ego; it was no problem to just walk into his parent's bedroom and nose about until he found what he was looking for.

Although the weapons were very heavy for a little lad of his age, Hardy Flower managed to swing and thrust with the long bayonet, using it as a sword. Then, to his delight, he managed to clip it on to the end of the rifle, enabling him to charge and stab at anything which was soft, like the pillows and the eiderdown. All the time the butt of the rifle was dragging along the floor.

When the warlike Hardy Flower had finished his charging and stabbing – 'just like the soldiers do,' he thought – he set about trying to remove the bayonet from the rifle. Up until then, everything had gone quite smoothly. The eighteen inches of 'cold steel' didn't budge, as Hardy Flower twisted and pulled. All his efforts were in vain as he pulled and tugged, but it was no use. Somehow or other, the 'sword' had to come off – before anybody came into the house! In desperation, he looked round for something to knock the bayonet off with. His eyes scanned the bedroom, willing something to help him remove the bayonet. In one of the corners of the bedroom stood a very sturdy Victorian chest of drawers. The two small drawers at the top of the chest were private. The one on the right, belonged to his mum and was where she hid her private bits and pieces, such as her marriage certificate, a gold watch, a silver thimble, old family photos, and a secret hoard of chocolate. So, priorities first, a chunk of chocolate went straight into Hardy Flower's mouth.

The drawer on the left, however, was a different proposition. This belonged to his father, Mr Hardy Thomas, and it was always kept locked. Hardy Flower, the brat of a son, knew by heart what was kept 'locked up'. There his dad kept his treasured First World War medals and the rent money (which he always paid in advance). There, too, was his army service discharge book, his family and war photos, a minute tea tin, with a piece of his and his wife Flower's wedding cake, all saved for posterity. And last but not least, the drawer held his boot repair 'snobbing' kit, including a hammer. Could this be the answer to the 'fixed bayonet' problem? It seemed quite a natural thing for Hardy Flower to nip downstairs and grab the large bread knife, and somehow force the mortise lock open. The knife was the only thing which he knew would slide in between the drawer and the frame. His mum always had an old kitchen chair in her bedroom, which came in very handy for the now-panicking Hardy Flower to stand on, to do his bit of illicit 'locksmithing'.

The sharp edge of the carving knife bit into the brass bolt section of the lock, and with a quick twist of the knife, and to Hardy Flower's delight, the drawer was unlocked. His next move was to open the drawer, but the drawer was flush with the framework, and the handle was broken, so the heavy knife came in handy once again, as a levering jemmy. Perhaps, Flower Hardy mused, he had been a burglar in a previous life. Or perhaps it could be his future vocation? Armed with his dad's boot repairing hammer, Hardy Flower leaned the rifle and bayonet against the chair, and sat on the edge of his parents' huge bed. Then, having made sure he was comfortable, he held the hammer in both hands and swung it as hard as he could against the smooth round end of the bayonet. It didn't budge so he gave it a real hammering and still it still didn't move. There was only one answer: he would leave it on, and perhaps his brother Cliff would think he himself had left it so.

The bolt action on the rifle intrigued Hardy Flower, and as he played with it he thought how fun it would be to load it with the real bullets which were in one of the ammunition pouches of his brother's equipment. The clip of five bullets was very shiny and the brat of a boy knew that they had to be pushed into the magazine. What he didn't know was that they had to be pushed out of the spring clip as the magazine was filled, leaving the clip empty.

Pushing and struggling to push the bullets into the magazine was to no avail; he just wasn't strong enough and his hands were sore. Then Hardy Flower thought: 'I'll use Dad's hammer! They should hammer in; they've got points, just like nails!'

It was good fun, pushing the point of the bullets up and down, on the spring of the magazine, but they just wouldn't stay down. This meant that he would have to knock them in with the hammer. Holding the clip of ammunition points downwards on to the magazine spring, the innocent kid raised the hammer to smash the bullets in.

Smash! Bang! Wallop! Hardy Flower was so engrossed in his activities that he didn't hear anybody come into the house, until he heard, ... 'Oh my giddy Godfather! Good Gawd a'mighty!'

This was followed by a head-spinning and ear-ringing 'backhander', which knocked Hardy Flower sprawling across the bed. It was one of the hardest swipes he'd ever had! Though little did he realise it, there were still many to come in the future.

'Oh dear, oh dear, oh dear! You little bugger! Tut-tut! Can't you leave anything alone? You nosy interfering little sod!'

Hardy Flower's dad and his brother Cliff had come and caught him 'in the act'.

'Good Gawd!' bawled his dad. 'Look at where he's got it pointed, laid against the chair pointing at the bloody door! My Godfather's boy! You could have sent me and your brother to kingdom come! And I'm not ready to meet my maker yet! You'd better bugger off before I really give you what for! Gert'cha!'

Hardy Flower very hastily slithered and slid from the bed, dodging along the upstairs landing, to run down the stairs. He had on several occasions, been on the receiving end of his dad's back-handers, followed by the return of his palm, both of which rocked his head from side to side. Hardy Flower's best bet, after receiving a belt round his head in those days, was to keep out of the way, until his dad had completed his next 'shift' at work.

Later that the same year, when Hardy Flower's three brothers were all serving in the armed forces and were at home together, there was an air-raid with hundreds of German bombers flying high above. Guided by the River Thames they were heading for London.

There were so many aircraft in the sky, it was obvious it was going to be a long air-raid. The Thomas brothers Cliff, Ken and Jim, involved their youngest brother Hardy Flower in their horseplay. Unfortunately for him he had to stand like a statue on a ball-bearing, to be thrown and pushed from one brother to another. Then one of the brothers didn't catch him in time and the young boy fell past and out of reach of the stretched arms, resulting in an egg-shaped bruise on his forehead. There was a heart-rending cry, followed by copious tears. By some miracle, a large bar of chocolate was put into Hardy Flower's grubby little hands. And, of course, it was all blamed on Adolf Hitler.

Food became very scarce, so that when Hardy Flower was hungry he went scrumping for apples and pears. Sometimes he'd sneak into the garden and cut a small cabbage to eat, to get rid of his hunger pains. On other occasions he'd eat raw potatoes. The forever hungry and skinny boy eventually got quite a taste for raw vegetables.

Mr and Mrs Thomas's neighbour, Mrs Battershill, was a kind lady. Daisy and Hardy Flower very often stood by an adjoining gate and sang out, 'Good morning, Mrs Batts!' The kind and sympathetic neighbour, a kindly soul, often threw a bag of broken biscuits over the garden gate. More often than not, Hardy Flower managed to scoff most of Daisy's share before he ate his own.

The adjoining gate was convenient for the neighbours to pop in and enjoy a quick cup of tea and a gossip. On the odd occasion, Daisy and Hardy Flower popped in to see whether there were any errands to run. The twins called the old lady Mrs Batts because they couldn't pronounce 'Battershill'. Mrs Battershill was a well-off widow of an army sergeant. She lived with her brother, a Mr Fitt, and it always amused her neighbours to think of her maiden name being 'Miss Fitt'.

The old lady had a pet monkey, which, when it was out of its cage, was a very spiteful animal. It scratched and bit the twins if it couldn't have its own way. It screeched and chattered as it raced round and round the room, tearing at curtains, knocking things over in its temper, being more spoilt than a baby. Hardy Flower and the chimp just did not get on, especially when Hardy Flower ate its sweets and nuts when the old dear wasn't looking. The monkey died eventually, probably from starvation if Hardy Flower was anything to do with it. With a lot of wailing and sobbing, Mrs Battershill went to her neighbours for help. But the only help they could give her was the offer to bury it, which she accepted. Only too pleased to be rid of the 'stinking smelly enemy', Hardy Flower volunteered to dig its grave. But first a miniature coffin had to be made. When the animal was laid in its box, a tin of lime was shaken over it, which Hardy Flower – grave-digger that he was – couldn't understand. Then, to make it a proper funeral, the old lady insisted that her neighbours attend the funeral, to say a few prayers and to send her pet on its way to heaven.

A month later Hardy Flower, the brat, sneaked into Mrs Batt's garden and dug up the monkey's skeleton and hung it by its neck from a tree using two broken bootlaces. The tree, of course, was well away from his own back garden.

Mr Hardy Thomas always went for his beer on a Sunday dead on twelve noon. For as many years that the twins could remember, he had his first pint in his club, called The Invicta, and afterwards, at one fifteen precisely, he would walk into The Old Prince of Orange, where he stayed until the pub closed at two o'clock. One Sunday afternoon, after Mr Hardy Thomas had had his drinking session, followed by a heavy roast dinner, and before going to bed to sleep off the beer, he gave his orders to his two eldest sons, Jim and Ken, who were still at home at the time. (Ken was eighteen and Jimmy was seventeen.)

'Jim, get the washing-up done!'

In the Thomas household there was only a cold water tap over a shallow sink. If hot water were required, water had to be boiled, or else the greasy washing-up had to be done in cold water. Usually the older brothers delegated the task to the twins to do between them.

Later on, Hardy Flower sneaked upstairs to look at and to listen to his dad snoring, but his dad was awake and as the peering boy looked round the bedroom door his father snarled, 'Has Jim done the washing-up, boy?'

Of course, Hardy Flower answered in all innocence, not wanting to be lumbered with the horrible greasy dishes in cold water.

'No, Dad!'

Then he hastily went back down the stairs. He had seen the flint-like look which had appeared in his father's eyes, and that look meant instant trouble for someone.

Suddenly there was a noise on the stairs, as streaking down the stairs wearing just his long johns came Mr Hardy Thomas the father. At the bottom of the stairs, in the small hallway, he grabbed the unsuspecting Jim, who didn't have a clue as to what was happening.

Mr Hardy Thomas grabbed his third son by his collar and hissed: 'You little bugger! I told you to do the washing-up!'

Then, without further ado, he punched his son on the head. For all of his seventeen years, Jim had always stood and taken those many 'good hidings'. But Jim was growing up, and on this occasion he turned on his dad, and their arms started to swing here, there and everywhere as father and son number three fought their way along the passage to the kitchen, where Jim's brother Ken decided to join in. Although no blows seemed to be meeting their mark, arms and legs were flying about in all directions, like windmills in a strong wind. Ken, the eldest of the two brothers, stood back far enough to take up a boxer's stance and performed what he thought was a boxer's fancy footwork. Not wanting to hurt his dad, Jim allowed his fist to go everywhere without connecting, and as he pulled them back his elbows came round to block his dad's punches. There was no chance of any of them really getting hurt. Mr Hardy Thomas, the 'shitter-flap' of his long johns dropping open, was up in the corner and sliding about in his socks, with a big toe poking through. As he went back against the wall, his feet slid forward, causing him to slide down the painted wall, while Daisy and Hardy Flower ran about like chickens and screaming their heads off.

Now Mr Fitt, the small and scrawny next-door neighbour, came running in, trying to stop the family scuffle as he patted the air around whoever was nearest. But he only got in the way and he had his spectacles knocked skew-whiff. This was no place for a skinflint watch repairer, striking at his neighbour with a rolled-up copy of yesterday's *Daily Mirror* which he had come in to scrounge. 'Papers are so dear to buy these days!' he'd whinge. Sensibly, he scampered away, but as he did so a ceramic pint pot – issued to Mr Hardy Thomas during his days in the First World War – came sailing through the open door. The hero Hardy Flower had thrown it, imagining that he was killing everybody, restoring peace and earning himself the Victoria Cross for valour. The missile hit the kitchen wall and shattered. The boy hero's 'hand grenade' had exploded with no casualties.

The incident fizzled out when Mrs Flower Thomas came on the scene, waving the soot-blackened flue brush in the fighting family's faces. Soot flew everywhere, and as the men slunk away in shame her only thought was for a cup of tea. For some reason, when something went wrong in the house, Mr Hardy Thomas would always look and point to Hardy Flower and say: 'It's all your fault – you – Hardy Flower! Yes it is! It-is-always-your-fault-boy!'

Hardy Flower's dad took great delight in repeating this until the boy ended up in tears. Sometimes the tears were followed by the back of his father's hand across his face, followed by another head-rocking blow as the palm made a return journey, back across Hardy Flower's other cheek. Perhaps the skinny brat deserved it – or perhaps he didn't. Although the 'double whammers' hurt, Hardy Flower loved his dad, though he did wonder why the six-feet giant had to keep swiping at him.

When Mr Hardy Thomas came home from work, either at two fifteen or six fifteen, depending on the shift, Hardy Flower would often be playing in the road at the front of the house. When he saw his father returning from work, he'd always run up to him, to hold his hand until they got home. Then when Mr Hardy Thomas had almost finished his dinner, Hardy Flower would invariably go to sit on his lap, hoping to get a taste of his dad's well-peppered potatoes and gravy.

By the time Hardy Flower was eight years old, he was wetting his bed every night. Unfortunately, the boy only got one change of shirt once a week, on a Sunday morning, and that clean shirt never left his back until the following Sunday, which meant he had to sleep in it, soiled on not. Hardy Flower wore short trousers, but never underpants. The warm itchiness which the damp shirt caused when he tried holding his tummy in away from the wet shirt was most uncomfortable, and the draught up his trouser leg made him shiver. By dinner-time, his pissy wet shirt would be dry but stinking.

Often when Hardy Flower arrived at school, he'd hear his teacher say, 'Somebody doesn't wash themselves before they come to school!?'

And Hardy Flower's best friend, Colin, would whisper in his ear:

'Your legs are dirty, and your hands, and your arms! Doesn't your mummy ever wash you?'

Naturally, the grubby kid stood up for his mum.

'Ain't got a mummy – I've got a mum, and it's because I've been playing on the school steps, and they were dirty!'

'But your legs were dirty when we came through the park!'

'I'm not dirty. I have a bath every Sunday!'

Every night, after his shirt had got wet and his bed soaked through, the bed cover was left open to dry, winter and summer. If it didn't dry, then Hardy Flower had to lay in it, as it was. It was an old bed, made with double sheets torn in half, and on top of the sheet he had either an old army blanket or some old coats which were no longer worn. Sometimes the sheets got washed. Sometimes they were thrown away.

Some good friends of Mrs Flower Thomas, who thought they were giving her some good advice, would say:

'Don't let the boy lay on his back. A good thing is to tie a wooden cotton reel on his back. If he lays on it, he will turn over, and it will relieve the pressure on his bladder.'

Hardy Flower thought he was relieving the pressure on his bladder quite well, without the use of torture. It was his first test of endurance, laying on the cotton reel, although it was to no avail and very uncomfortable.

Then his puzzled brain was subjected to even more terror.

'If you don't stop wetting the bed, you'll eat a fried rat for your tea – every night!'

For the confused boy, the problem wasn't wetting the bed;

it was the nightmarish remedies which were inflicted on him, which made the matter much worse! Then came another 'cure-all' - water torture.

'When he's asleep, put his hands and feet in a bowl of cold water. It will stop the dirty boy wetting his bed!'

This meant that Hardy Flower was sat up and subjected to a midnight dip. Eventually, he got to the stage where he became petrified and afraid to go to sleep at all. As none of the old wives' remedies ever worked, they petered out and his slumbers went uninterrupted for a further three years, despite him still wetting his bed every night.

The bedroom which Hardy Flower slept in was the height of luxury to him. Alongside the bed on the floor was a piece of lino to step on to when he got out of bed. Over his head, hanging from a fly-specked ceiling hung a solitary fly-specked light bulb with no lampshade, other than a fly-encrusted piece of flypaper. The curtaining was a strip of net on the bottom half of the window frame. To cover the whole window and keep out the draughts, as well as keeping the light from shining out at night-time during the air-raids, there was a half of an old army blanket, the corners of which were forced over a nail at each side of the window. There was another bed in the room, for any of his brothers who came home on leave from their military services.

Outside the bedrooms on the upstairs landing was a three-gallon enamel bucket, for anybody who felt the need to use it during the night. The bucket could stand empty for two or three days, but it always had a newspaper laid on top of it when it gradually filled up. The bucket got heavy, especially, it seemed, when Hardy Flower was told to empty it. He'd grab the thick wire handle and try to lift it, hoping to swing it forward on to the landing and along the linoleum towards the top of the upper four stairs. Getting the bucket down the stairs was a tricky business, as it had a wider base than a stair, so with a heave up and a push forward, the bucket went downwards, sometimes two stairs at a time. Eventually, the eight-year-old boy would get it to the bottom of the stairs, but then he still had to turn the corner into the hallway and bump down another two steps into the kitchen, before going out through the kitchen door. Outside the door was a high concrete step, alongside of which was the drain from the kitchen sink.

By the time he had reached that point, his arms felt as if they had been wrenched from their sockets. If nobody was looking, he tipped the bucket into the drain, rather than carrying on to the lavatory. There he'd have another Herculean struggle, trying to lift the massive great bucket up and over the edge of the pan. So it was inevitable that, more often than not, the contents of the bucket disappeared down the drain outside the kitchen door. Hardy Flower was well aware of how unhygienic this practice was, so he always let the kitchen tap run until he thought the drain was clean. Fortunately, he didn't get this arduous job very often.

During the Blitz there was one very bad night-time air-raid when the Thomas family hadn't been quick enough to get to the air-raid shelter, so they huddled together in the front room. They could hear the drone of the bombers heading for London and Tilbury Docks and the clatter of anti-aircraft guns as they fired into the sky from all around Gravesend and Tilbury. Bombs came hurtling down and exploded all round them. First they would hear a high-pitched whine, then a few seconds later there would be several explosions one after the other. On that particular night, there was an almighty explosion, and the windows were all blown in, but luckily they were taped. The soot from the chimney went all over the room, and when Hardy Flower put his shoes on, he cut his toe on a piece of the smashed mirror which had fallen into his shoe. That was Hardy Flower, war-wounded.

Both Daisy and her twin had a degree of damage done to their ears by the explosions and this resulted in them both having to attend the ear clinic every Monday, for months on end, sometimes waiting from early morning until mid-afternoon. There were many civilian casualties who had to attend all sorts of clinics in those wartime days. There were friendly mothers, with noisy kids, and friendly kids, with noisy mothers.

When a road was repaired it was done properly, and instead of a quick patch-up, the road was re-gritted and re-tarred. Gravel and flint chipping went everywhere, to eventually end up in the gutter, ready for Hardy Flower to kick everywhere, with one of his famous footballer's kicks. But on the way to school one morning, he got off to a bad start as he watched the huge steam-roller puffing its way backwards and forwards along the tree-lined St Thomas's Avenue. Hardy Flower loved the smell of the boiling tar as it was spread over the road with heavy rakes and brooms. Then, to his amazement, his mouth received a nasty wallop, and he wondered what had hit him as the tears streamed down his face. So intent on watching the steam-roller was he that he had been unaware of a tree which was in his path. He had walked straight into it, resulting in a fat lip minus one front tooth.

After school, he could hardly wait to get back and watch the steam-roller at work, and, to his joy, it was still in St Thomas's Avenue. At the kerb, however, a crowd of people stood staring at the sky and somebody shouted: 'Look! A barrage balloon has broken free!' It was always a sight for everybody to stand and stare at when a barrage balloon broke away from its moorings. The barrage balloon went soaring high into the sky, and everybody would watch, waiting for it to explode under the atmospheric pressure. Then they would watch it float gently down to earth like an exploded whale. As it floated out of sight, Hardy Flower stepped forwards to take a swipe at a neat pile of grit, but unfortunately his boot lace was undone, and the other boot was standing on it, which made the clumsy boy topple over on to the newly gritted surface. It was no problem. Very quickly Hardy Flower scrambled up on to his feet – after all, it was an everyday occurrence for him to fall over himself like this.

The show was over and the onlookers went on their way, but one voice spoke to Hardy Flower.

'You'd better get home, sonny, and get your hand seen to!'

When the young boy looked down, his hand was covered in bright streaming blood. It was only a one-minute run to get home, and luckily his dad had just arrived in from work. Mr Hardy Thomas showed a lot of concern at the blood dripping from his son's fingers, so he pinned a note on the door for Mrs Thomas, who was nattering to a neighbour, to say that they had gone to the hospital a mile away. Mr Thomas strode out in true military fashion, and the only way that his wounded son could keep up with him was for him to be dragged by his good hand.

After a wait in the casualty department, father and son were called in to see the doctor, who took hold of Hardy Flower's hand, twisting and turning it, first this way, and then that way, finally saying:

'Yes, it is a nasty cut.' Reaching for a pencil, he continued to speak to the boy's father as he drew a ring round the frightened kid's wrist. 'There's only one thing to do, and that is to cut the hand off, just on that pencil mark. Wait there, I'll just get my scissors.'

Hardy Flower was absolutely petrified to think that the doctor was about to hack off his hand with his scissors. Everybody was laughing; even his dad and the nurses thought it was amusing. A junior nurse arrived with a tray and whispered in the distraught boy's ear.

'If you come with me, dear, I'll soon make it better!'

The nurse was very gentle with his hand, and once it was cleaned and stitched up, she applied enough bandages to make it look as if it had been cut off.

'There you are! You can go now, wounded little man.'

Hardy Flower was on the verge of tears, wondering what

was going to happen to his hand after it had been cut off. 'Were they going to eat it?' the upset boy wondered. However, the nurse had told him he was wounded, so obviously, if that was what she had told Hardy Flower, then that was what the young boy would tell everybody else. 'I was wounded in the war!'

Humour in the war was high, but sometimes it could be cruel.

At eight years of age Hardy Flower was considered to be old enough to run the family errands. His regular weekly errand was to fetch the family rations and he always ran to the Co-op shop, though he never ran back because the shop was a half-mile away. With a ten-shilling note and a huge canvas bag, off he went to collect the rations for the whole family. The three adults' ration books were buff-coloured; Daisy's, Rose's and Hardy Flower's junior ration books were blue. If either of the elder brothers were on leave, then they would be issued with special food ration cards. The meagre rations would have to last the whole family for one whole week.

This particular errand meant that Hardy Flower had to walk along an alley between two overgrown and very old tennis courts. The alley led into the posh Woodfield Avenue, where two 'right little madams' lived, namely Jill and Audrey. They, jointly, commanded the Woodfield Avenue Gang, which, at full strength, could muster ten plump and well-dressed children. If they were referred to as 'children', they were posh. The twins were always labelled 'the poor kids' who lived in Park Road. The Park Road Gang had a complement of one – Hardy Flower.

The opposing gang leader, Jill, the chief 'little madam', was invariably accompanied by one of her 'lieutenants', and they always seemed to be in the alley when the lone boy was on his errand. To his discomfort, the gang's female boss was always armed with a long, tapered swish, cut from a shrub.

Jill the gang boss had quite a knack of swishing her circus whip round Hardy Flower's legs as she shouted:

'Where are you going, Hardy Flower Thomas, with that horrid and grubby shopping bag?'

The sting of the bully girl's lash on his bare legs always made the grubby kid dance and made him whinge.

'I've got to go for the rations, and my dad will be coming down through here in a minute!' He hoped that this would deter the vicious female gang leader from using her stinging lash, but she'd put her nose in the air and sniff disdainfully:

'Hardy Flower Thomas! I don't believe you! Your father is only a shift worker in a factory and he's at work!'

Then she'd slash at his bare legs, again and again, finally saying:

'You can go now, Hardy Flower Thomas, you dirty kid – you stink!' She continued slashing at his bared legs as the terrified boy ran for his life, and as he ran he held back the tears, because a girl had hit him.

Many times Hardy Flower decided to go the long way round, which would take twice the time, but at least it was less painful. He went each Monday to collect the rations, and the canvas bag was always full and extremely heavy, and the only way he could carry it was to sling it over his shoulder. As the bag was so heavy, he always decided to go the shortest way home, through the alleys and old tennis courts. By the time he got there he'd be well and truly weighed down with 'rations for six for one week'.

There was never ever any going back. As soon as he walked into the alley, much to his dismay, he was always surrounded. There was no way out for Hardy Flower, until he'd 'run the gauntlet'.

'You are a dirty kid! And you don't wash, and you always smell pissy!' hissed Jill, filled with hateful glee. 'So you must be punished! And you can turn out that dirty old shopping bag! Come on! Turn it upside down, or else we'll all thrash you!'

So the poor dirty kid had to tip everything out and allow his family's one week of rations – the jam, butter, bacon, sugar and vegetables all to be passed around the gang.

Then Jill shouted with glee. 'As I thought, you stinking filthy boy! No soap or toilet rolls! You filthy wretch! Yuk! Put it all back, before we catch something from it, you smelly kid!'

To their sneers and catcalls, Hardy Flower bent over the bag to repack it, and as he did so, Jill, needing to unleash her power of captaincy, gave several hard slashes with her swish across the back of his bared thighs.

'You can go now,' she screeched, 'and don't let me catch you in our gang's territory again, you dirty stinking kid!'

As Hardy Flower scraped and bowed to her, trying to go past, Jill gave him another slash across his bare legs. The injured boy's attitude was changing and he had murder in his heart, but his altered looks warned the little vixen gang-leader. She nodded to her cronies, who immediately pushed and jostled their victim.

'Yeah!? Yeah!? Get going, you scruff-neck kid and don't come into our alley again!'

With the aid of kicks, thumps, and more shoving and pushing, Hardy Flower's path was suddenly clear. With legs bruised and smarting, his mouth dry from fear, and his heart pounding, he heaved up his mum's home-made canvas shopping bag and made a dash for home, which was less than fifty yards away, running hell for leather up a concrete slope and finally into Park Road, as if he was climbing out of hell.

Once Hardy Flower was into 'his' road, all was forgotten. He daren't tell anybody about those incidents because of the stigma of being frightened of a girl and of not standing up to the gang.

Jill, the gang leader, eventually got her comeuppance. On her way home from school one day, she was knocked down by a bus and, although she wasn't seriously hurt, her face was scarred for life. One of her cronies was killed in an airplane crash when he was seventeen; he was training to be a pilot in the Royal Air Force. Another one of the gang became a famous TV comedian, while her fat bullying brother rode roughshod over everybody on his way to a top executive position.

Jill's gang had a rallying call – a piercing whistle which they performed by blowing through two fingers. If Hardy Flower ever showed any sort of resistance towards her, when she was having a go by herself, she just whistled, and he would always find himself surrounded by her 'heavies'. The call sign for Jill's gang was 'Yah! – Honky-ho-o-o-olay-ee-dee-oh!' Very often Hardy Flower could hear the gang's call sign while playing in his garden, then he'd think to himself: 'All the kids are playing together again, I wish I could be one of them.'

The kids in the bullying gang lived in the lower half of Woodfield Avenue. The kids from the upper half were snootier and never come down to 'the lower level'. The Woodfield Avenue gang boss was a year or two older than Daisy and Hardy Flower, as were most of her cronies. The twins went to the same junior school as they had, but eventually the whole gang went to the local grammar school. This was about the same time that Daisy and Hardy Flower went away yet again.

The kids from the upper half of Woodfield Avenue tolerated Jill and her gang, but their mothers had told them not to talk to those two 'poor kids' from Park Road – they are so dirty! And, naturally, the kids tipped their heads back, and looked down their noses when they passed the twins.

When he was ten years of age, Hardy Flower 'fell in love' with a little girl from the snootier end of Woodfield Avenue. She was always so clean and pretty and always wore a crisply ironed blouse or dress, surmounted by her golden hair which was always neatly brushed and tied with a coloured ribbon to keep it in place. One thing the young Hardy Flower always noticed was the fact that she wore lace-edged knickers, as opposed to the drab and dismal knee-length 'all-weather' knickers. Every time the grubby kid saw golden-haired Rita, he hung around – he wanted her to be his sweetheart, though doubtless her mummy had said: 'No, darling, stay away from the children in the alleys, especially the boy who smells!' And she did. Nobody could blame her either – especially when the ammonia fumes wafted up her nostrils from his damp and pissy shirt.

Rita Pudmen eventually went to the grammar school with another very pretty girl, who would later turn Hardy Flower's head when he reached the age of fifteen. This was Miss Brenda Walkwell, who had been in his first infants class.

6

The Blitz Continues

The war continued as everybody continued to dive for the air-raid shelters when the sirens started wailing their message of impending danger. The looks on everybody's faces, and the thoughts that showed on them, were tense, as the bombs whistled down, and the anti-aircraft guns fired at the enemy airplanes. That look of apprehension would ask: 'Are we safe, or is this it?' Everybody was apprehensive and full of doubt.

On wet and windy autumn days the children loved walking to school through the Woodlands Park and watching the autumn leaves blow from the trees, and gently float down, sometimes landing on a pool of water. The children would pretend that they were boats, then Hardy Flower would splash about, trying to sink them. This always made him late for school, and he and a few other kids were always late back after the lunch break, too. School lunch-time was twelve noon until two o'clock, and the children who were late back after the lunch period were always punished, sometimes with so many hundreds of lines to write, like 'I must not be late for school' or 'I will not linger in the park and make myself late for school!' complete with the correct punctuation marks.

Quite often, the children would receive corporal punishment, the nature of which depended on the teacher's mood, and what they favoured at that particular time. A popular one was for the children to hold their hands out, palm uppermost, then the teacher would use their favourite weapon, for instance a twelve-inch rule, to strike the children right across the fingers, level with the tip of their thumb. Fortunately, the pain soon wore off. Sometimes the teacher would use a cane, of which there were a variety. Long, short, fat, thin, smooth or knobbly, they all had one thing in common – they hurt like hell. Most of the teachers had their favourite.

Some of the vicious blows really hurt, leaving the hands bruised, but nobody ever said anything. If a kid was disobedient, then they were punished, both at home and by the teacher. The worst punishment Hardy Flower received was 'two on each hand' and an order to stay behind after school and write five hundred times: 'I will not mock my teachers!' Those punishments pulled most children into line, and possibly made some of them into good citizens. Some children, on rare occasions, had a finger broken with the cane.

One particular day the children returned to school for the afternoon and settled down for their ten-minute 'sleep time'. Miss Rouse, a young teacher, had gone to the back of the classroom, probably to warm her bottom on the radiator. Always an inquisitive little boy, Hardy Flower grew curious as to what his young and pretty teacher was doing. With his head laid on his folded arms on the desktop, he very slowly raised his elbow and peered underneath it, towards where his teacher stood. What he saw made him open his eyes wider. The newly appointed young lady infants teacher was standing against the radiator with one side of her skirt pulled up to her waist adjusting her stockings and suspenders. Unfortunately for Hardy Flower, she looked up and saw him gaping and leering at her. She dropped her skirt and leapt forward, a look of thunder on her face. The prim young miss swiped Hardy flower round the head, knocking his face against the top of his desk.

'Turn your head round and face the front, you nosy little wretch!' she snarled. 'In fact, you can stand outside the classroom door. It is quite cold out there – it might cool you down, you filthy little swine!'

The teacher grabbed Hardy Flower's ear between her finger and thumb and dragged him into the corridor – much to the delight of the rest of the class. It was cold standing in the corridor, but Hardy Flower was in for some entertainment. As he leaned lackadaisically against the wall, suddenly there was a lot of commotion inside the classroom, so Hardy Flower had to sneak a look – the fretful young teacher was at it again, giving somebody else a sound thrashing. Through the window he could see that the teacher had another boy out at the front of the class, gripping him by his wrist with his arm straight up, forcing him to stand on his tiptoes. As Hardy Flower watched, the irate teacher slapped the boy on every part of his body, especially on his bare legs, arms and face. She wasn't just giving him a 'sound thrashing', she was beating him up. When 'Miss' had finished venting her rage, she gave the beaten boy such a shove that he ended up knocking a chair over as he fell under a desk, screaming his lungs out.

That lady teacher, probably not even twenty years old, was crying herself. Was it out of rage? Or perhaps she had lost her boyfriend or father in the war? The children heard afterwards that she had been reprimanded by the head teacher for being too harsh, though the children didn't understand the meaning of 'reprimanded'.

On one memorable day during the Battle of Britain the coalman and his horse and cart were in Hardy Flower's road. The road had recently been tarred and gritted. It was on a lovely summer's day, and the tar was still soft with a lovely strong smell rising from it. As usual, Hardy Flower was inhaling the tar fumes on the kerb. As the coal-man's cartwheels ground through the grit and came towards the grubby boy, he thought to himself: 'I could hang on the back of the cart and nick a ride!' But, his mother had other ideas for her youngest son.

'Hardy Flower! – I want you to go to the butcher's for the meat rations. I want a pound of mince and some sliced corned beef … and don't forget the change!'

At that particular moment, Hardy Flower was enjoying himself and didn't want to be interrupted, so he went into an immediate sulk. He just didn't want to go all the way to the butcher's – it was at least a half a mile for him to walk and he wanted to play about round the back of the horse and cart, especially as this particular horse always seemed to have a pee in their road, which amused the kids.

Normally, he'd get a clip round the ear, and be sent on his way, and no arguing. However, this particular day Hardy Flower's mum was in a hurry and instead called on another boy, Leon Tartle, who lived opposite. The boy didn't very often come out to play, but Mrs Flower Thomas was desperate, as her husband was expecting his dinner.

'Of course I will go for you, Mrs Thomas,' the sneaky little swine answered. And off he went, with her one-shilling piece, leaving Hardy Flower quite free to play about in the road and watch the coal-man's horse have its pee. Sometimes, it relieved itself completely, and the waiting boy would have to beat the neighbours to the steaming pile of manure with a shovel and bucket, which he would then spread round the tomato plants. His dad would give him a penny for the muck-spreading.

By the time the street sneak Leon Tartle arrived back from the butcher's, the coal-man and his horse had completed their deliveries and disappeared. The sneaky Leo, returning with the goods, called out, in his best grammar-school voice:

'Here is your mince and corned beef, Mrs Thomas!' Just as if Hardy Flower wasn't there.

Mrs Flower Thomas took the package. 'Thank you, Leo, for going. You can keep the change, as you have been such a good boy!'

As he passed Hardy Flower, he smirked like the sneak he was. Hardy Flower shouted after him:

'I'll get you, you four-eyed private school kid!' – all the while thinking to himself: 'I could have had a bottle of lemonade, or a hot meat pie, and even some cakes with that change!' He knew that, even if he had run the errand, he wouldn't have got the change.

Leon Tartle grew up to be a stalker and a flasher, often doing his business while hiding under a steel railway bridge. He was caught exposing himself while looking up through the iron steps at the girls as they walked overhead. He didn't return to Gravesend when he was released from prison.

Hardy Flower had forgotten about the mince and the change, until thirteen years later, when he would be in a dodgy and somewhat uncomfortable situation fighting the EOKA terrorists in the Troodos Mountains of Cyprus. Suddenly, through his mind flashed the thought: 'If I had gone for Mum's mince-meat, she could have bought another fourpenny-worth of mince with the change! If I get out of this little mess, I'll never, ever, refuse my mum anything, ever again!'

That same year, while Hardy Flower was standing 'on guard' at the front gate, armed with a home-made sword, a wooden rifle, complete with his mum's carving knife tied on the end for a bayonet, a strange lorry appeared along the road. Until then, the only lorries to come into their cul-de-sac were for the delivery of coal, logs or paraffin; anything else would be delivered by horse and cart, handcart, or a tradesman's three-wheeled delivery bike.

'It's the Germans! They've come for me!'

Panic surged through Hardy Flower's young mind as he hid behind the ferns in the front garden. There were three men dressed in strange uniforms of a kind he had never seen before – they wore trousers and jacket joined together at the waist and thick heavy glasses which stuck out from their heads. Surely they were the enemy! Hardy Flower drew his sword and stood ready to charge into the men if they came too near to the gate.

The 'enemy' uncoiled a roll of rubber tubing and clanged some heavy-looking 'bombs' on to the roadway, as Hardy

Flower watched in awe. Then they set light to a long brass thing, which roared with flame as they squeezed the huge trigger. Suddenly, the boy jumped out of his skin, as a great stream of sparks hurtled towards him. As he fled indoors to get his mum – *she*'d soon sort them out! – the 'Germans' went into guffaws of laughter.

The 'Germans' were workmen, of course, sent to burn down the iron railings using oxyacetylene iron-cutting equipment. Hardy Flower watched the rest of the 'invasion' from the front-bedroom window. He enjoyed watching the sparks fly everywhere and seeing the molten lead poured into any holes left in the brickwork or the walls, to prevent people catching their fingers in them. All the scrap iron was collected for the war effort and melted down to make guns, ships and bombs. Nine years later, Hardy Flower would be using the same equipment as an apprentice boilermaker plater.

There were still some wrought-iron railings to be seen in the town, round basement steps and cellars; they were left there for safety. People cared for one another in the dark days of the war.

Having defended his family and home and had an adventure, Hardy Flower decided to drift off and find his friend Harold.

Harold Everett lived in the next road, and he and Hardy Flower went to school together. His mother had died when he was seven. Harold and his dad lived in a small terraced house. Halfway between Hardy Flower's and Harold's houses was a cakes and pie shop, and everything cooked in the shop was delicious and always made Hardy Flower's mouth water. To get to Harold's house, Hardy Flower had to pass the front of the pie shop, where his friend's dad was the baker.

Harold and Hardy Flower were sitting in the tiny parlour, wondering what to do with themselves?

Suddenly, Harold said with pride, 'I've got a money box!'

'Oh yeah?' Harold's little friend Hardy Flower thought to himself, thinking inwardly of freshly baked pies.

81

'But I can't reach it,' continued Harold. 'It's up there, on the top of the cupboard.'

Hardy Flower looked up. 'Aha!' he thought. 'There it is.'

On top of the shelf stood a miniature tin post-office savings box, for children to save their money. It did seem to be quite high up but not quite out of reach! Hardy Flower's devious little mind was rapidly working overtime.

'I'll get it down for you!' And as fast as a starving cat-burglar, he stepped on to the settee armrest, then climbed up the shelves as if it was a ladder.

Having grabbed the money box, the lithe and hungry kid tucked it into the top of his jersey and climbed down, then very generously he handed the savings tin to his friend Harold, as if it was a gift. But Harold seemed quite nervous, so Hardy Flower decided that, as he had made the effort, he should be rewarded for his daring act. Harold started to speak.

'Hardy Flower, I don't...'

His friend butted in. 'I'll show you how to get some money out. Get the bread knife!'

Grabbing the bread knife, Hardy Flower slid it into the slot and quickly turned the well-filled money box upside down, then, 'Bingo!' – first time! Out slid the jackpot – pennies, sixpences, halfpennies and shillings. Gathering up the coins, he did the decent thing and handed them to his friend Harold. 'After all,' he thought, 'they are his!' Once again, and before the coins could be put back, Hardy Flower shinned up the furniture and replaced the money box.

'Come on, Harold, let's go and buy some pies!'

Harold stood there with his mouth opened wide in amazement, not too sure of what to do, but as Hardy Flower was so adamant he agreed. So off to the cake shop they ran. On the way, they bought a large bottle of lemonade each, then went into the cake shop, for hot pies and fresh chocolate and cream cakes.

Fully loaded with bags and bottles, they headed for the

local park, where they could sit and enjoy their goodies, which Hardy Flower considered, at the time, he had well and truly 'won'. But they never made it. Halfway to the park, they were stopped dead in their tracks. Harold's father had stepped out from an alley to stand directly in front of the two boys.

'Hello, Mr Everett.' Hardy Flower ventured, in his friendliest and most polite voice.

'Be quiet, you!' Mr Everett was angry. He had been in the back of the baker's shop, and, unknown to them, he had seen Hardy Flower buy the pies and cakes. Then he had watched to see which way the two boys went, and then took a short cut through the alleys, to confront them.

Mr Everett knew his son's friend and where he lived. He also knew that there was no way on God's earth that the wretched boy would have money to buy what they had just bought, and he himself didn't allow his son Harold, to have money to waste. He didn't say anything to Hardy Flower, but to Harold he quietly asked:

'Where did the money come from, boy, to buy these things?'

And, of course, Harold told his father the truth.

'Out of my money box, Dad.'

That was it. Mr Everett looked Hardy Flower up and down, and spoke sharply.

'You! Take the lemonade and the pies, and go straight home with them.'

Hardy Flower just couldn't believe his luck. 'What, all of 'em?'

'Yes, boy, all of them!' hissed the irate baker. To his son Harold he said, 'Go home and stay there until I get back!'

Hardy Flower really couldn't believe his luck: two large bottles of lemonade, four hot pies, and a bag of cakes. This lot had cost all of one shilling and ninepence – a fortune! So he took off and he'd scoffed the lot by teatime.

Hardy Flower thought that his friend Harold would be

interrogated and punished? But Harold just received a telling-off and a friendly warning from his father. However, from then on, 'that boy – Hardy Flower' was never allowed inside his friend Harold's house again.

There were some occasions when the hungry kid kindly did go to the butcher's for his mum, a half a mile up hill for fourpenny-worth of corned beef, the meat ration for the week for four adults. He went with a one-shilling piece. The errand always took Hardy at least an hour, because he was a dawdler, unlike the sneaky Leo Tartle who ran there and back. Standing in the queue, Hardy Flower liked to watch as the butcher picked up a seven-pound tin of corned beef, chopped the end off the tin with his meat cleaver, then pierced the other end of the tin, to let the air in. Then the huge lump of corned beef plopped on to the butcher's block. His mother's meat order was usually nine slices, which the butcher wrapped, first in a piece of grease-proof paper, and then in newspaper. And there would be threepence change. On the way home, Hardy Flower crept into the nearest alleyway and very carefully unwrapped the paper to remove three slices of corned beef. 'After all,' he thought, 'a growing lad has to keep his strength up to run the errands!' Each slice was the size of a paperback book cover, and as thick as a two-shilling piece. The brat ate the three slices of corned beef as fast as he could because he was so hungry.

Getting nearer to home, Hardy Flower had to pass The Prince of Orange pub, where, just outside, stood a posh-looking weighing machine. All that had to be done was to push a one-penny piece into the top slot and watch it roll downwards to activate the mechanics of the scales. Hardy Flower had always wanted to weigh himself for a penny and now was his chance. Anyway, wouldn't his mum let him keep the change from the meat rations? With this in mind he weighed himself three times with his mum's change, but threepence was threepence in the war days.

When he arrived home, his mum asked him for her change, and Hardy Flower – very much the brat, told his mum that the butcher hadn't given him any. Mrs Flower Thomas was not at all amused. She wasn't at all money-minded, but it was hard to make ends meet, without being robbed of threepence by her scoffing son. Her ham-like arm raised itself, as she pointed a straight index finger towards the butcher's shop a half a mile away.

'Back!'

There were no ifs or buts.

In the butcher's shop the boy whinged: 'Mum sent me back for the change!' And for some reason the butcher just handed it over, trusting the hungry-looking lad to be telling the truth. After Hardy Flower had got the change he was to go and buy three one-penny postage stamps – 'Or else!' He was always a hungry, lying brat of a boy.

Much later, the still-hungry kid pulled the same stunt with the 'Spam' ration, but this time he returned the change to his poor mum who, he thought, never ever found out. Hardy Flower didn't realise that he was cheating on the rest of the family. Real hunger could make a boy do almost anything.

On his eighth birthday, Hardy Flower was not wearing any shoes or socks – socks were an ill-affordable luxury anyway. His mum was in a very bad mood because it was washday. The whole week's washing was done on a Monday by hand, which meant everything, including everybody's socks. This meant Mrs Flower Thomas was extremely busy. Because it was his birthday, Hardy Flower was asking for some lunch or dinner; it was all the same to him just as long as he got something. But there was nothing and he cried out to his mum that there was never ever anything to eat.

While Hardy Flower was getting 'lippy', his mum was poking the washing down into the copper boiler, using the copper stick which was a piece of a tree branch, about thirty inches long. The weekly dip of the stick into boiling water

Leabharlanna Poibli Chathair Baile Átha Cliath

Dublin City Public Libraries

and Oxydol soap flakes had bleached this cudgel white. Suddenly his mum turned on him.

'Right, my lad! Eight years old, and getting lippy already, are we?'

There was a steely glint in Mrs Flower Thomas's eye. She'd never had this from her other four kids, and she didn't intend having it now, especially on his birthday! Eight years old and *demanding* his dinner!

Up went her sleeves, pushed right up passed her ham-like elbows, and her look alone was a sure warning, and punishment enough! As if to say, 'I'll give you bloody dinner, boy!'

Hardy Flower knew what he could expect. It was too late to run away, because his mum had positioned herself, between the wash-house door and her mouthy son. Through very thinly pursed lips, Mrs Flower Thomas hissed at her son.

'I'll teach you to get lippy with your mother, you little bugger!'

Nobody, ever told the young boy what a 'bugger' was? He thought back then that perhaps it was a bug catcher.

The cudgel-shaped tree branch-cum-copper stick, seemed to travel in slow motion as Mrs Flower Thomas aimed it at the body of her lippy son, and Hardy Flower yelped as it found its mark. He tried desperately to dodge her other huge flailing arm, but he had got his mother's 'gander' up, and she was after him, still swinging the piece of tree branch.

Dressed in his usual basic manner – just a jersey and short trousers with no undergarments topped with a 'tar-brush' haircut – shorn up the back and sides, with just a bunch above the forehead, the birthday boy ran indoors and through the kitchen, trying desperately to dodge the issue of 'whack!' 'thud!' and 'thump', and that was only in the kitchen. Through the hall and up the stairs he ran. His mum was certainly letting off steam with her 'cudgel'. Along the dark upstairs landing and into her bedroom Hardy Flower ran as his cudgel-wielding mum flayed the air with the blunt weapon as her

86

birthday boy dodged round the end of her bed. Whack! Whack! There was no let-up, as Mrs Flower Thomas vented her fury. He could tell from every blow that his mum really meant it.

Feeling the worse for wear, Mrs Flower's youngest son had had enough and made for the door, haring off back along the landing, slipping and sliding down the stairs, as he tried to escape his mother's wrath. At the bottom of the stairs, where he thought he was safe, he looked up the well of the stairs and shouted out to his mother, who was peering down at him with murderous intent.

'I'm telling Dad about you when he comes home!'

But Mrs Flower Thomas was still not finished, for her answer was to send the copper-stick-cum-cudgel hurtling down like a rocket. It whizzed past her sweet son's nose before hitting his big toe. Hardy Flower thought his toes had been broken off and with one loud yowl he made his final retreat. Hardy Flower didn't get away with being lippy, and he certainly would never, ever, forget his eighth birthday.

On another wash-day, Hardy Flower came home from school for his dinner. Again his mum was at the copper, sorting out the washing.

'Is there any dinner for me today, Mum?' Hardy Flower asked.

'No, you'll have to wait,' was the curt reply.

The skinny kid went into a sulk and sneaked off upstairs, where he lay down under his bed. A short while later, he heard his mum shout out to Daisy.

'Go and find your brother!'

Hardy Flower rolled right over to the wall, so that he couldn't be seen. Seconds later he heard Daisy calling out, 'He isn't up here, Mum!' And off she went.

It was terrible for the hungry boy, lying under the bed in the thick dust and fluff and getting it up his nose. It made him want to sneeze, and that would have 'blown his gaff'.

Sneaking out, he crept back downstairs, having given up on any thought of getting some dinner, so he decided to go back to school. But when he had got as far as the local park he continued his sulk there. It was then that Hardy Flower decided to run away and join the Royal Navy. He was wondering whether he could be a sailor, now that he was eight years of age, when suddenly Daisy came along and shouted in her bossiest voice: 'Mum's got some dinner ready. But you will have to hurry because it is nearly time to go back to school!'

Hardy Flower decided to go back, just that once, and give his mum one more chance! Dashing all the way back, with the thought of dinner on his mind, he called out happily:

'I'm back, Mum! Can I have my dinner?'

Mrs Flower Hardy's answer was very curt. 'Yes! It's on the table!'

On the table was a very thick 'doorstep' sandwich, and for Hardy Flower to be able to eat it all, it was necessary for him to part the two slices and take a bite at one of the corners. The filling was a thick layer of cooking lard, his 'fat ration' for the week.

Having partaken of his lunch, the well-greased boy made a run for school. It was at least a mile away but he didn't quite make it in time, and along with the other naughty kids he lined up to take his punishment, which was two strokes of a twelve-inch rule on the back of the knuckles.

Hardy Flower never looked forward to Monday wash-days: it meant 'stick' at home, and 'stick' at school. Real wooden sticks, not verbal!

Mrs Flower Thomas always prided herself on the fact that her boys and girls were 'always rough and ready'! It sounded good to her perhaps, but one day much later Hardy Flower would sit and think about it and conclude: 'Rough and *weak*, more like.'

Hardy Flower's first memorable embarrassment also took

place during the lunch break. He had rushed home from school, knowing that his mum's cousin, Auntie Beatrice, would be there with her new baby. They were all there, sitting, drinking tea, and chatting. The baby was being made a fuss of and of course there was no dinner ready for the twins. By the noise the baby was making, it was obviously feeding time – for her. Once again, the hungry young boy asked for his dinner. His mum and her cousin whispered and then burst out laughing. Suddenly, Aunt Beatrice's hand disappeared inside the front of her dress, and there, in front of Hardy Flower's nose, was a massive great white balloon thing being thrust at him. At the front of the balloon was what he thought was a very large strawberry. His Aunt Beatrice laughed and asked him: 'Would you like some titty then, Hardy Flower dear?'

Pulling on the massive mammary, the new mum jerked it all out, letting her hand slide towards the big strawberry, with the intention of feeding her baby.

The skinny kid who always looked all head and ribs was all eyes and open-mouthed, as he stared at something he had never knowingly seen before! Then came shock and horror as a stream of warm milk hit the back of his throat. The startled boy coughed and choked, but the joke was on him as the baby glared at him while she clamped her bare gums on to the massive big strawberry. Hardy Flower's face was crimson and burning up as he hung his head in shame. After the teasing had stopped, he enjoyed a thick slice of bread and jam, then he fled back to school.

After that experience, Hardy Flower's heart would always start to race at the sight of or on contact with a large, warm and blue-veined female breast. But not always in horror.

7

Hardy Flower Helps the Midwife

Christmas was always a very exciting affair, though it was hardly mentioned until, at the earliest, two weeks before.

Christmas 1942 was a very white one, and a Christmas song had just been released called 'White Christmas'. That Christmas was just like the song sounded, because everywhere was under a carpet of crisp white snow. The luxury of Christmas was to have a roast chicken for dinner, or, if a family were lucky, a huge joint of beef. Christmas Day was the only time the children had an orange, which they'd find in their Christmas stocking along with six brand-new pennies, a handful of sweets and a small toy from Woolworth's, which sold nothing more expensive than sixpence.

Most families stocked up with huge bottles of beer, a bottle of whisky, and a bottle of sherry for the ladies. Although there was a war on, and things were rationed, booze from under the counter was available for 'cash'. The nosy and inquisitive boy, Hardy Flower, always took a sip of everything, and whatever it might be it always left a nasty taste in his mouth.

On Christmas day, everybody gorged themselves, attacking the large roast chicken with gusto. The working classes made the most of the festive season because nobody was ever off work for more than two days other than at Christmas. Christmas was celebrated for what it was, and not for 'how much?' or 'how big?' or 'how many?'

Most children received just one toy for Christmas, which had to last them until their birthday. Most toys were made of wood or tin; plastic was unheard of. When the toys got broken or lost, most children made their own fun and games. Hardy Flower's particular artistic talent was for making a home-made bow and arrow or a sword. They were the weapons which helped him defend the top of the air-raid shelter against Daisy and her friends, or cats and dogs.

One of the neighbours had a cat which had a long shaggy and possibly diseased fur, and it liked to creep round, on the lookout for titbits. To Hardy Flower, the cat was a ferocious lion. When the 'lion' was on the prowl, he become a Zulu warrior, his spear a very worn-down garden fork, with prongs very short and sharp. Suddenly, the 'lion' would put in an appearance as it stalked up the garden path, looking for its 'prey'.

Taking aim, the skinny-ribbed and half-pint-sized 'Zulu' heaved the four-bladed spear into the air, just like the Zulus did in the film *The Four Feathers*. 'Clunk!' – it came down, pinning the cat's tail to the ground, though luckily for the cat the prongs landed each side of its tail. The 'ferocious animal' was held there, pinned to the ground and roaring like a lion. The hunter, who himself looked like a starved alley-cat, all head, ribs and shinbones, had been brave enough to throw the spear, but afterwards he was frightened out of his skin as very tentatively he took a broom and jogged the fork free, just enough to allow the cat to tug its tail free and escape. Hardy Flower, the famous big-game hunter, daren't go near it for a long, long time.

The king of the castle loved the garden, with his castle battlements high up on the top of the air-raid shelter. In his surrounding kingdom was a very large Victoria plum tree, a Cox's Orange Pippin apple tree and, at the bottom of the garden, was a William's Bon Chrétien pear tree. Very often, Hardy Flower climbed the pear tree, only to find he couldn't get back down, which meant he had to stay up in the tree until his dad lifted him down, resulting in a ' double-hander'.

When the king of the castle was big enough to scramble down quickly, he made a garden swing and a 'Tarzan' house in the big pear tree. The swing was his mum's washing-line with an old motorbike tyre tied on the end. An apple tree spanned the next-door neighbour's shed roof, making it too easy for the skinny and agile kid to climb up into and steal the windfalls. Unfortunately, once his jumper was filled up with apples, it was almost impossible for him to move – resulting again in the hungry boy being left there – 'until your father gets home!' Hardy Flower had got quite used to the 'double-handers' which his dad dished out. The actual punishment for him was the waiting and the threat of 'a bloody good clout'!

In this home-made adventure playground was a huge tin bath which Daisy and Hardy Flower often sat in. They would stick their mum's brooms over the sides and the bath would become their boat. Once a week, the bath was taken inside and filled up with hot water, always on a Sunday morning. Then, according to their position in the family pecking order, everybody would take their turn, warming it up with saucepans of boiling water from the kitchen stove.

At the bottom end of the garden were lots of bushes, with old pieces of wood and corrugated tin sheets. These Hardy Flower used to make his second, more secret camp, hidden away in a corner. There, too, propping up the rickety fence was a huge steel bed frame, made up of lots of coiled springs, all secured inside a soft wire mesh. By supporting each corner with old metal buckets and bricks, Hardy Flower and his twin sister Daisy had the time of their lives bouncing up and down. Some kids from the gardens backing on to their garden would climb to the top of the fence and sit looking in awe at some of the things which Daisy and Hardy Flower got up to in their 'adventure playground'.

During the early autumn of 1942 Mrs Flower Thomas had to stay in bed. Each day a very strict nurse came regularly to the house, while Mr Hardy Thomas was at work. Rose and the twins would be sitting in the kitchen, having come home from school for their lunch. While they carved the bread and smeared it with dripping fat, the local midwife was upstairs, attending to their mum. Suddenly, the midwife came rushing down the stairs, shouting at them: 'Get lots of boiling water ready, as soon as possible!'

None of the children had a clue as to what was going on. Hardy Flower stoked the kitchen stove up with coal and got a lively blaze going, then it wasn't too long before there were kettles and saucepans full of boiling water ready. As they waited in ignorance, the midwife came down and told the children that their mum was staying in bed for the day. 'You three children had better start carrying bowls of hot water upstairs and leave it outside the bedroom door!'

Laden with bowls, jugs, saucepans and a kettle, the three children did as they were told, until everything which could hold water stood on the upstairs landing. They hung about in the kitchen, making toast and dripping fat, until the nurse come down and spoke very briskly to Hardy Flower.

'Here, boy! Burn this in the stove and poke it down and make sure it burns away!'

The nurse handed the wide-eyed boy a bloodstained bundle wrapped up in newspaper, while his two sisters looked on in horror. Hardy Flower was in charge of the fire, so he pushed the mysterious blood-soaked package into the flames, poking and prodding at the hissing and sizzling bundle until it had disappeared.

Several minutes later they heard the cry of a baby. Rose, Daisy and Hardy Flower sat there huddled together, mouth agape and eyes wide open, not knowing what to do, not even comprehending the situation. Then the midwife appeared to tell them that they now had a little baby brother. Of course, the first thing Hardy Flower thought was: 'Good, we can stay off school! And then he thought: 'And it means there will be another ration book, a baby's green one this time!' Immediately in his head he 'bagged' the new baby's sweet rations. But unfortunately for him new babies didn't get a sweet ration; they had a special ration of concentrated orange juice.

Rose and the twins hung about at home, during that September lunch-time, until they had seen their new baby brother. It was even worth being late for school and getting their hands caned. There was no excuse for bad timekeeping.

Instead of a gas mask, the same as everybody carried, their new baby brother had a rubber 'gas chamber', into which he would go if the Germans ever dropped gas canisters. The gas chamber had a visor with a flat, flapping snorkel tube to enable the baby to breath, and when the babies were put into it they screamed their tiny lungs out. By law, everybody, including children, had to carry their gas masks with them wherever they went. Hardy Flower couldn't understand why new mothers didn't carry the big rubber gas chambers with them when they took their baby out.

Some nights, when it seemed as if most of the Luftwaffe had come over to bomb London, Tilbury Docks and the munition factories in Gravesend and Northfleet, it was unfortunate that a lot of bombs fell on and around Gravesend with several bombs falling on private houses. Most people spent the night in the air-raid shelters, cold, miserable and hungry. They had heard the bombers coming, high in the sky, and following the course of the River Thames. After the bombs had been dropped, the bombers turned to make their return journey to their airfields in France or Germany.

Soon after, the 'all-clear' siren was heard and everybody climbed out of the air-raid shelters, cold, stiff, tired and hungry. As the shelters emptied, each person went about their daily business, just as they would have done after a heavy shower of rain – the men went to work, the women shopped and did their housework, while the schoolchildren went about their learning or mischief, depending on their mood. Everybody felt tired, but it was just how things were.

One such morning, after a particularly nasty air-raid, Hardy Flower was up early for once. His dad had gone to work and his mum had the new baby to feed, which meant, for the twins, no 'cat's lick' – a quick wipe over the face with the dishcloth – and no breakfast, which was usual anyway.

On his way to school, going the long way round, via the local park, Hardy Flower decided to call for his friend Malcolm who lived opposite the park. If they were lucky, they would have time to look for shrapnel, fallen from the exploding shells or bombs high in the sky, and sometime stray bullets as well. But Hardy Flower was in for a disappointment. As he got nearer to his friend Malcolm's house, which was situated on a corner at a crossroads, there seemed to be a lot of action going on. The long lanky boy reached the end of the fence, then he saw the house, or where it had once stood, before it had been blown to pieces by a German high-explosive bomb.

His friend Malcolm's house had disappeared, and in its place was a massive heap of rubble out of which drifted a spiral of dust and smoke. Hardy Flower walked over the site of warm and dusty debris, and then all around it, hoping to find his friend Malcolm. He couldn't see him anywhere, and Hardy Flower started to call out, 'Malcolm! Malcolm! Where are you, Malcolm?' Yodeladio!' He ended with their secret call sign.

Looking round, the suddenly frightened boy could see shoes and books, with bits of clothing, crockery and furniture, lying about just as if a high wind had blown it all there. Air-raid wardens, a policeman, ambulance men and several neighbours were digging into the rubble, some using garden spades and forks, and some using their bare hands. Smoke and dust drifted on a soft breeze, gentle enough to carry away departed spirits. An old tramp from the park opposite was foraging in the upturned dustbin. The family's bath lay at the bottom of the garden, its plug still swinging on its chain.

There was no sign of Hardy Flower's friend Malcolm because he was dead, and so were all his family. Their house had received a direct hit and had been blown to smithereens. An air-raid warden, red-faced old Mr Mawbey, the local pushbike specialist, saw Hardy Flower and whispered very quietly.

'If you are looking for Malcolm, son, he's dead. You had better be getting off to school now, or else you'll be late!'

So that was it. No farewell and no tears. That was life in wartime, or the loss of it. All the kids went to school as usual, and for once, and once only, they were not caned for being late. Later in the week the school had a special prayer service for Malcolm Hewson, a little lad whom Hardy Flower had liked because he was very much like himself. They had been the very best friends.

The war went on and on and on. The air-raids continued, and Mr and Mrs Thomas were getting more and more worried each time the air-raid siren sounded. Then, all of a sudden, it was decided, once again, that their twins, Daisy and Hardy Flower, should go to Gloucestershire, but this time to stay with Mr and Mrs Jones and their family of three boys. These were the Joneses who lived in the old servant's quarters of their Granny's old cottage in Whitminster. Their gran was just too old and tired to look after them now.

It was to be their third evacuation, and the twins were still only nine years old.

Part II

8

Joyous Race to the Ragman

Daisy and Hardy Flower Thomas were going away again and because they had outgrown their previous going-away clothes, which were in tatters anyway, they had some new clothes bought on 'tick'. Daisy had a new rain mac, a set of underwear, a pair of socks, a new frock with a two new white ribbons for her hair. Hardy Flower had a new overcoat with long pointed lapels which soon started to droop like a sad dog's ears. Because the lapels were pointed they annoyed the highly strung boy, so he began to chew them to shreds. Also bought for him were – to his young mind – two of the most ridiculous-looking boy's caps, which were pleated round the crown with a squared peak held together with a press-stud. He wouldn't have minded if they had been normal schoolboy's caps, like most boys wore. Perhaps they were the height of fashion and probably Mrs Flower Thomas was doing her best for him. But there was no way *he* was going to wear those 'stupid nutcase caps!'

Just before they were due to be evacuated to Gloucester again, Hardy Flower and Daisy's dad soled and heeled Hardy Flower's boots, with a new layer of studs. Their father earned many a 'pint or two' mending other people's boots and shoes – often referred to as 'snobbing'. Hardy Flower decided that 'if my dad can do it, so will I!' And he would!

The week when the twins were due to go off to Gloucester again, the ragman stood outside their school gates hoping to exchange his toys and children's books for any old rags. The twins raced home as they always did when the peddler put in an appearance. Out of breath after running home, they half expected the usual refusal, but their mum relented and allowed them to gather up their recently discarded and threadbare clothes and take them back to the ragman. Overjoyed that they could be like other kids and collect a small toy, the twins forgot all about their lunch-time bread and dripping, and with a cry of 'Race you to the ragman!' they hastily ran back to school, three-quarters of a mile away. For Daisy and Hardy Flower Thomas, it was a joyous walk home from school with Daisy carrying a small ragdoll, and her brother a toy tool set which consisted of a hammer and nails, tiny wooden blocks and a cardboard pattern to nail the blocks to. The next day they would be going away.

Once again, the twins left their mum indoors with a long drawn out 'Ta-ta, Mum!' and tears in their eyes. Off they went to the station, and in all probability Mrs Flower Thomas was feeling tearful as well. It was a very hard decision for their parents to make, sending their children off to live in another part of the country and for goodness knows how long?

Once again, the twins stood on the railway platform with their father. Hardy Flower was wearing his dog-eared coat and carrying his two new caps, with his boots newly soled, heeled and studded as if he was going mountaineering. It was a wonder he could lift his feet as he slid about on the platform. Tied in their lapels were huge brown parcel labels with 'WHITMINSTER–GLOUCESTER' printed across them.

The twins had nothing else to carry, and if they should be fortunate enough to have a bath, their clothes would have to be washed at the same time and dried in front of the kitchen fire in their new home. *If* they should be so lucky!

On the way to London, a huge man got on the train, and

the passengers, began to whisper that he was a German spy, probably because somebody had said that people belonging to the German race were heavily built.

Because the twins were evacuees, they were allowed special passes to travel on the railway free. When they arrived at Whitminster, Daisy and Hardy Flower were quite reluctant to go with Mr and Mrs Jones – their grandmother's neighbours, who were to be their new 'foster parents' – because there was always a spiteful-looking smirk on Mr Jones' lecherous face. Eventually, their father persuaded the twins to go and play with the Jones boys, which they did, not really having any other choice, and once again their dad disappeared and the twins were on their own.

Mr and Mrs Jones lived in the lower half of their gran's cottage. Originally the lower half on the end of the cottage had been a cellar, then later it had become the servant's quarters. The Joneses living room was the old outhouse and the top part of the outhouse formed their sleeping quarters, which was entered by climbing a short ladder. The mattresses covered the whole of the sleeping area, with Mr and Mrs Jones sleeping on the right, and their three boys on the left. There was another door which led into the garden. The top half opened, while the bottom half could be left shut. Up in one tiny corner was a space just big enough for Hardy Flower and Daisy to lie down in. For the small sleeping space and their keep, Mr and Mrs Jones were paid the statutory allotment of money for evacuees.

Their first day at their new 'home' was all fun and games, but once their father had disappeared Mr Jones became the 'lord and master' – 'Mr and Mrs Jones to you'm two!' Hardy Flower wondered why Mr Jones was forever taking his heavy old leather waist belt off and flicking the soft end round his and his sister Daisy's bare legs. Mr Jones would laugh his head off, as they scuttled up the small ladder, shouting after them: 'Argh! The next toime oi'll use the buckle end! Ooh-argh! We'm'll soon have you'm a'skipping ter ouwerrr tune oi'll wagerrr!'

When he spoke, his face was would be set straight and stern. Daisy and Hardy Flower huddled up close together, absolutely petrified.

Hardy Flower often sneaked a look back down into the room where everything apart from sleeping happened – the cooking, eating and general living. One time he saw Mrs Jones sitting in front of the old-fashioned kitchen range, talking to her husband.

'You'm shouldn't froighten those chillun's loike that, Tah'm,' she whispered.

As she was whispering, Mr Jones' bony hand went up her skirt and immediately Mrs Jones giggled.

'Ooh argh, Tah'm!' said Mrs Jones, now panting heavily and with breasts heaving. 'But they'm be a watching ... ooh arrgh! Oi'm ready, Tah'm!' she gasped. 'You'm best see'um off, Tah'm ... Oi'm a' comin', Tah'm! – Oi'm a' comin! Ooh Arghrrrr!' And Mrs Myrtle Jones flooded profusely into her cowhand husband's grimy palm.

The young and innocent Hardy Flower listened as he watched, thinking 'Coming?' but she's already here! Once again there was a cruel smirk on Mr Jones' face as he brutally buried his four gnarled and calloused fingers deep into his wife's moist and receptive love nest and reamed quickly and mercilessly before withdrawing. As he turned away from his wife he looked towards where he knew the young boy was hiding and with a twisted smirk, Mr Jones quickly sniffed at the glistening mucus which was rapidly cooling on his fingers, then reached for the buckle of his heavy leather belt with his other hand.

'Gerrtt-cher!' he snarled, whipping out the well-worn strip of leather with a crack like a pistol shot. 'You'm'll git a taste o' the buckle-end a'gin, moi lad, you'm wait un'see if'n you'm daw'n't!'

102

And the watching boy fled.

Mr and Mrs Jones had three sons, Fred, Dick and Harry. Fred was a few years older than Daisy and Hardy Flower, while Dick was two years older than the twins and Harry one year younger. The three brothers took after their mean-minded and spiteful father, copying everything he did. Although their stay with the Joneses wouldn't last as long as their stay with their Gran, the twins suffered some distressing and traumatic moments.

Once again, Daisy and Hardy Flower went to the village school, and there was the same atmosphere. They were still the strangers or, perhaps, intruders. They both tried to be friendly, but unfortunately the regional dialect remained a barrier.

Often, Mrs Jones' father would arrive at his daughter's house for dinner on a Sunday, especially when beef was on the table. He was a small man, with a head of pure white hair and a large white moustache, and seemingly kind, but he just didn't like Hardy Flower. He always made the timid boy eat food which he knew the boy didn't like. Hardy Flower couldn't stomach turnip and swede and half-cooked meat fat, and, much to the young boy's embarrassment, the white-haired old man always watched him closely during the meal and always passed comment. Sunday lunch-times, when they were all sitting round the table, a plate was put in front of Hardy Flower and straight away he thought, 'I can't eat that!', 'that' being a huge, thick slice of grisly and fatty undercooked beef. He had eaten the roast potatoes and some of the root vegetables, but pushed to one side the swede and the huge wedge of fatty beef which he knew he couldn't handle. The old man watched the sad, pale kid pick at his dinner, then he started to pick on the boy.

'Un what be wrong wi' tha meat, and tha'se vege-doubles?' he'd snarl. 'You'm dawn't get down from the table until you'm eaten un all. Oi'm a'going to sit y'ere, and watch un

103

until all that food is eaten! We'm can't afforrd ferr yeh ta waste it loik ye do's at hawme! Spoilt ye be, Oi knaws yey ad a soft an' easy loife, it shaw'se, but we'm cun soon alter yeh!' Old Gramps Jones was a belligerent man, despite his kindly looks.

Everybody sat there staring, amused, while Hardy Flower ate the dinner under duress. He sat with his back to a roaring fire, feeling completely hemmed in, gagging on every mouthful as he forced it down. The meat being sinewy and not cooked right through made his stomach heave, but when he tasted the beef fat he almost puked. Of course, old 'Leather Belt' Jones thought it was all hilarious. Afterwards, Hardy Flower had to ask him: 'Please may I get down from the table, Mr Jones?'

The Jones boys had long gone out to play, but it was always the same: Mr Jones would make Daisy and Hardy Flower wait, especially if he could see that the boy wanted to get out for some fresh air. When they were eventually given permission to leave the table, Mr Jones would rapidly take hold of his thick leather belt and, as the twins walked past him towards the door, would flick its end at them with an evil grin spread all over his face. For the umpteenth time he would ask: 'Which end do'ee loikes – the leatherrr end orrr the buckle end?' Both the twins carried welts and bruises from the leather waist belt.

During the following months Daisy and Hardy Flower would suffer a lot of humiliation – and not only at the hands of Mr Jones.

When they had first arrived, the weather had been quite cold and Hardy Flower remembered the warm spring and summer days when they had stayed with their Gran next door. But now when they played in the fields Daisy and himself were always at the beck and call of the Jones boys. Daisy Thomas, not wanting to be far away from her twin brother, wanted to join in the games, to which the Jones boys readily agreed. Like their father, they had a streak of ignorance and cruelty in their make-up. Daisy joined in the rough and tumble of the boys' 'games' but she was to suffer very nasty experiences. The Jones boys, not having a sister in the family, became very curious about young girls, wanting to know how they were built, and what made them different from boys – 'They'm b'aint got no cock… What did gurrls piss frum? And whoiy did um sit down to do un?' Eventually, the Jones boys became more and more inquisitive, because now there was always this girl playing in their field.

Out of sight of the house, the Jones boys became adventurous, very often bullying Hardy Flower into keeping a watch-out while they played 'Doctors and Nurses'. It was during those games that Daisy's body was spread-eagled and held down by the boys who examined her genitalia by prodding and poking her with sticks and twigs. Hardy Flower, forever under threat of being beaten with sticks or the kids' bony fists, cowered, frightened out of his young wits. The 'pretend' doctors enjoyed their anal and vaginal examinations, and thought it was all a huge joke.

The twins found very little sympathy for their plight, even from their Gran. She simply wasn't interested – after all, 'Little boys dawn't do that sort of thing, do they'm!?' But, the Jones boys did. In all probability, their gran had had enough of children, having borne ten of her own.

An uncomfortable game for Daisy and Hardy Flower was to be the Jones boys' chariot. Daisy stood with her hands behind her, with Hardy Flower bending over double. Daisy was the horse and Hardy Flower the chariot, and the Jones boys would leap on to his back like three jockeys and make the twins run round the cow field, encouraged with a whip made from their father's broken leather boot laces. The knots hurt and stung the skinny 'horse' boy. The twins always ended up falling over, just to get the boys off their backs, though it was never long before the 'game' began all over again.

The misery continued when 'Old Jonesy' wanted a barrow load of logs picked up from a farm, and Hardy Flower had to take the part of the horse, his load being the three boys. It was a mile along a country lane to the log pile which always made him quite out of breath. The Jones boys loaded the barrow to about half full and decided between themselves that, as Hardy Flower had pulled the barrow going, then he could have a ride on the return journey.

Hardy Flower really thought his luck had changed as he clambered into the huge box on wheels and sat down on the logs.

'Lie down and have a rest,' laughed the eldest of the three.

'This is good,' Hardy Flower thought. 'I'm one of the boys now.'

'Go on, lie down and have a rest!' shouted Harry.

So the apprehensive and nervous kid lay down, then, much to his surprise, the lid of the barrow was thrown into place. He didn't like it one bit, so he tried to push it off, but to no avail, because one of the boys was sitting on top of it. Off they went, with the Jones boys laughing their heads off. Unfortunately for Hardy Flower, the barrow had been used for carrying agricultural lime and as it was pushed and pulled along the country lane the bumpy ride disturbed the lime, making Hardy Flower's eyes stream with tears and his skin smart. His 'ride' was horrendous and when he was finally let out, the Jones boys had the biggest laugh they had had in years.

'It's what they'm boys get up to, b'ain' it?' scoffed Mr and Mrs Jones.

The terrified evacuee boy never got the lime washed off but eventually it wore away. Little did he realise that he was born to push, but never to ride.

A pleasant period for the twins was the 'up with the sun, and down with the sun' at haymaking time. During the wartime years, there was a 'double summertime', especially for the farmers. The clocks went backwards, and forwards, giving the farmers more daylight at the end of the day for gathering in the crops. At haymaking time, everybody in the village was involved. During the day the farmhands cut the hay, and during the evening every family turned out to make hay while the sun shone and to clear the fields ready for ploughing. And even Gran and Gramps walked out and climbed the stile into the hay field beyond the top of their garden. All the children ran about while the adults raked up the hay and the tallest among the farmhands loaded up the great hay waggon, which was over twenty feet long. When the hay wagons were fully loaded, they looked like a haystack on wheels. Sometimes Hardy Flower stood on the cart and spread the hay very evenly, though whether he was allowed to do so depended on who the farmhand was. The ever-hopeful boy usually climbed on top of the hay wagon when his Uncle Tom was the spreader.

Hardy Flower liked to lead the big shire horses who moved the cart around the field. Sometimes there were two, rather than just the one, it depended on the size of the cart. He loved the smell of the horses and the hay in the evening sunshine and the way the sun reflected off the horse brasses as they clinked on the polished leather. Haymaking could be a very hot and dusty job, so, to make the evenings more pleasant, flagons of apple or pear cider were placed under the hedges at various spots around the fields, alongside bundles of fresh crusty bread, farmhouse cheddar cheeses with the rind still on, and huge juicy onions. At any time, anybody could help themselves to a snack.

Hardy Flower didn't know about the cider until he was chasing round the field with the friendlier kids, when suddenly he spotted a flagon poking out from under a hedge. 'What's this, then?' He let the other kids run on, then reached down to drag the earthenware bottle out of its hiding place. To his surprise, he heard a moaning sound coming from the other side of the hedge. Naturally, Hardy Flower looked closer because all he could see so far was the open end of a feed barn. It frightened the small boy to think that somebody or a helpless animal could be lying there injured or in pain. He peered into and past the hedge, getting a clear view into the feed barn where to his surprise he saw his 'foster mother', Mrs Myrtle Jones, leaning forwards over a bale of hay. Her skirt was pulled up and over her hips and behind her was a young farm labourer, fully mounted, much to Mrs Myrtle Jones' evident delight. Hardy Flower swallowed because he could see that the man who had crept up behind Mrs Myrtle Jones seemed to be pushing a sausage in and out of her bottom and it seemed – at least to his innocent mind – to be hurting her because her mouth and eyes were opened wide as she moaned and groaned. He wondered why the man didn't even stop hurting her when she asked him to stop. 'Ooh arrrgh! Oooh arrrgh! Ooh God! Ooh! Ooh! Ooh! Don't ... stop! ... Don't ... Stop!...'

At that point, Mrs Myrtle Jones, the 'village bike' since she was fourteen, and her lover seemed to have exhausted their pent-up energy, and collapsed, as at the end of a pretend wheelbarrow race, into the bale of hay. At this precise moment the boy sneezed, causing the startled lovers to duck down out of sight, hoping the sneezer wouldn't notice them. On the opposite side of the hedge, Hardy Flower sneezed again as the dust drifted over from the hay field and went up his nose. The thirsty kid removed the stopper from the flagon and took a sniff, thinking to himself: 'What a daft and silly way to have a wheelbarrow race, and then fall over!' The lovers had disappeared and, as Hardy Flower liked the smell of crushed apples, he tipped the flagon cider over and filled the tin cup which hung from the handle by a piece of rough twine. He drank two cupfuls, then put the stopper back quickly.

Suddenly, he felt very, very dizzy and sick, his knees wobbled and his head started to ache. He didn't feel at all well. Then the sky started to spin like a whirlpool and his balance was gone. He tried to walk forward but his knees buckled, making him fall down in the long grass where he immediately fell into a deep sleep. What he had swallowed was the farmhands' 'rough scrumpy', the workers' original home-made thirst quencher. The nine-year-old evacuee was tipsy.

The sun went slowly down, and as the summer heat cooled, Hardy Flower woke up none the worse for wear. The haymakers had reached the bank of the canal and now sat talking and smoking while they passed the bread and cheese and flagons of scrumpy round. Their haymaking day was almost over. Hardy Flower sauntered along, and because he was a loner nobody seemed to have missed him. At the edge of the hay field close to the canal bank were all kinds of birds flying about. Rabbits, hares and game birds ran for their lives as the hay cutter went to work, and several haymakers waited with their shotguns – the evening sport would help supplement their dinner tables with rabbit stew, game pie and rich and dark jugged hare.

Various types of birds, blackbirds and sparrows flew here, there and everywhere. Uncle Tom kept two jackdaws as pets at home. In the trees and in the air flew several wood pigeons, owls and other woodland birds, their variously coloured plumage flashing through the different greens of the countryside.

Mrs Myrtle Jones was again taking advantage of the double-summertime evenings, having grabbed herself a tall and handsome young farm labourer, and hastily pulling him behind the last haystack. With her back against the soft and warm hay Mrs Myrtle Jones relaxed and received her young lover, letting her knees bend down and outwards. The two pairs of knees relaxed and started to tremble just as Hardy Flower strolled towards the lovers. He didn't notice the hasty pulling down of her dress.

Mrs Myrtle Jones took her lover's head in her hands and

looked into his eyes. 'Therr you be, young J'arge. B'ain no more 'un a green floy in yore oye, but he'm be gone now, and so must you get you'm salf hawm or your'n motherr will be a'frettin. Off you'm goes now whoile I takes young Harrdy Flowerr haw'me. He'm be toired out.'

The young lover, no more than sixteen years old, moved off, and like dozens of other young men from the parishes round Whitminster he was head over heels in love with Mrs Myrtle Jones.

Hardy Flower couldn't understand why Mrs Jones, his so-called foster mother, was being so nice to him.

'If you'm dawn't say nutten to anybody about me helping that pore boy with a floiy in his oye, oyl give you'm two kids a piece of choc'lut when we gets haw'm!' Then to cover herself the wayward lady hastily added: 'But if'n Oye 'earrs you'm told anybody a'tall, Oi'l tell Old Jonesy – yes! We'm baw'th knaw's you'm calls 'im "Old Jonesy" an' he'm dawn't loik it! So if'n you'm says owt 'bout the floy in young J'arge Buckmasterr's oye, Oi'l tell him you'm be a'loi'in and fer 'im ter tak' his buckle-end to you'm an' yorre sisterr!'

Hardy Flower was being dragged back over the fields to the cottage, and as he was so terrified of the buckle end of Jones' belt, he answered: 'I promise I won't say nuthink to nobody, Mrs Jones!'

Mrs Jones smiled to herself. She was safe.

'You'm moight get two pieces of choc'lut when we'm get's haw'm, little loverrr!'

In the public bar of The Whitminster Inn 'Old Jones' knocked back his fourth pint of Shire Bitter, thinking to himself: 'One morre an' Oi'l be gettin' back to cover moi Myrtle, but firrst Oi'l make sure they'm Lunnon nipperrrs are awake and scare the shit out'ern 'em with a flick o'me strap ter let 'em knawss Oim hawm, and, ter let that young shaverr watch, seems ter get moiy ouwld 'oman a'goi'n, it do!'

And so, exactly thirty-three minutes later, after receiving a weal-raising slash from the swishing strap, Hardy Flower lay behind the heavy curtain which separated the bedroom from the small cottage parlour. He wasn't disappointed when Mr and Mrs Jones started 'doing it' with slaps of Mr Jones belt and Mrs Jones giggling 'Ooh arrrgh! Tah'm – Ooh arrrgh!'

Mr and Mrs Jones' love antics made Hardy Flower open his eyes wide, and put his hand over his mouth and recoil in horror and disbelief at what he was seeing. And when Mrs Jones' mouth opened wide, gasping out unintelligible words and Mr Jones' eyes started to stare and grow bigger, Hardy Flower backed away from beneath the curtain and crawled under his side of the musty-smelling blanket. The welt on his buttocks was beginning to sting.

Very often a discarded horseshoe, which a 'hunter' had shed, would be picked up by the country children with glee; it was considered to be lucky. Most of the children collected a lot of rubbish from the fields, like horseshoes, and horsehair, rabbits' tails, and coloured bird feathers, which they made their fishing floats with. And they selected the many-coloured and different-shaped leaves, with some wild flowers, to press in their bibles. Very often the twins saw the local hunt drinking from the 'stirrup cup'. Then it was off to cries of 'tally-ho!' and the poor 'hard-up' gentry engaged in full pursuit of the fox. When the exhausted animal was finally torn to bits by the hounds, its tail would be cut off and the remains of the fox would be stuck on a hedge or fence, as a warning to any other predatory and carnivorous wildlife. Sometimes there would be a dead badger slung on to a barbed wire fence, left to rot.

The lonesome twins often lay down on the banks of the canal and gazed into the crystal-clear water, watching the various fish darting in and out of the reeds. Sometimes they were able to catch some, but the sticklebacks always seemed to disappear from their jam jars. Very often they caught perch and roach, cutting their fingers on the sharp barbs on the fins. Along the canal banks, they ran after butterflies, and dragonflies, trying to make a collection to pin on to a board. The catching and collecting were done on a friendly basis, but when it came to whom they belonged to it was possession that was nine points of the law. This always meant that everything belonged to the Jones boys, at least after a few threatening thumps.

Daisy and Hardy Flower were frightened out of their lives once again when a farm labourer called at the house with some rabbits which he had caught with the aid of a stoat. The bunnies were dead, but the oaf put his hand into the sack and brought out a stoat, waving it in their faces. 'Moind it daw'n git ye! This'un loikes ter boite you'm kids from down Lunnon way!'

The terrified twins fled as the poacher and the Jones family roared with laughter.

One day their crippled Gran sent them mushrooming, saying, 'Awnly get the big thick black hoss-mushrooms as big as a dinner plate, moi deearrs!' The old lady made lots of mushroom ketchup, which she gave away. On their way round the fields they also had to collect any loose horsehair, which could usually be found on the thorny hedges. Their gran told them that the horsehair was to wrap round warts or unwanted spots, until they disappeared. The twins also picked and ate the leaves of the hawthorn. In the Gloucestershire countryside the yokels called it 'bread and cheese'. They chased grasshoppers and sometimes stopped to eat the red-and-yellow flower known as bird's-foot trefoil, though the local villagers called it 'egg and bacon' because of the colours.

Daisy and Hardy Flower often played in the field with a kitten, which at the time seemed to be their only true friend. They both wanted to hold it and stroke its fur though Hardy Flower's turn always lasted longer than Daisy's. One time the kitten suddenly scratched the boy's hand just as Daisy was insisting it was her turn. This enraged Hardy Flower and in his rage he threw the kitten at Daisy, quite gently, but Daisy was frightened, as the kitten sailed through the air towards her. The very young kitten let out a pitiful mew and spread its claws. Unfortunately for Daisy, all four sets of claws gripped the front of her jumper as the kitten desperately clung on to her. Daisy was hysterical and Hardy Flower thought it was hilarious – until, that is, his old adversary, Miss Matilda Shepherd, cuffed the back of his head, calling him a 'stupid boy!' The twins were still treated as outsiders, but two old ladies always welcomed them into their tiny thatched cottage on the bank of the canal. One of them was Mr Jones' mother, 'Old Great Granny Jones', while the other was a cousin who lived with her. They both wore long black dresses down to their feet, and both wore woollen shawls. 'Old Great Grampy Jones' for some reason lived and slept in the woodshed and was very rarely seen. The twins did hear the he was mad, but the old ladies spoke about the old boy suffering with shell-shock, caused by his service in the trenches during the Boer War.

Although the old ladies' cottage was small, the garden was immense, being a typical old country garden containing every soft fruit bush and every fruit tree imaginable. Quite near to the cottage was a natural fresh-water spring covered over with an old shed. One end of the shed was open, with ivy growing down to the three rocky steps leading to the clean, clear water. Hardy Flower had a quick look in there one day, being curious, and once again he was caught in the act of being where he had no right to be. Luckily, on that occasion, he was only warned that 'if he ever went down those steps again, the mermaids who lived in the spring would leap out and grab him, and take him down into the depths of the cold spring water, where they would probably eat him!'

On Saturday nights the villagers gathered in the local pub, while the children played in the yard at the back, eating their bags of crisps and drinking lemonade. When adults and children got into their individual groups, somebody usually got picked on to be talked about, or 'put on the spot', for the amusement of the others. Daisy and Hardy Flower were, for once, not left out, and very often they went to the village pub, always being told to 'walk round the corner, and play with the other kids', which was easier said than done. On those occasions, Daisy and Hardy Flower had to go wherever they were guided, pushed or shoved, but they went with good intent, wanting to be accepted and to join the kids and play games. But they spoke differently, and they were 'intruders'. The village kids were hostile and found 'they from Lunnon' hard to accept. One brave little girl smiled sweetly and asked Hardy Flower whether he still had any meat-paste sandwiches which he could swap. He didn't recognise her from the village infants' school the previous year.

Hardy Flower thought that he and his sister Daisy would have been better off dodging the air-raids at home, where at least they would have been able to have run home to their parents. The days and weeks went by, and still the twins didn't have much to do with their Gran and Gramps next door. They had been on their third 'evacuation' for almost a year and they wondered whether they were ever going home again. They had got quite used to taking the stick and running the gauntlet whenever they were confronted by the village gang. They had become hardened, but their natures remained that of loners.

Quite unexpectedly, one weekend during late summer, their dad paid a visit to his mother, their Gran and Gramps. To their great delight, their dad told them that they were going home with him once more. Perhaps Mr and Mrs Jones had had enough of them. Dressed in their Sunday best, and all ready to go, their father made the twins go back into the Jones' house on their own, and say:

'Thank you for looking after us, Mrs Jones! ... Thank you

for looking after us, Mr Jones!'

But their weak and pitiful words of thanks fell on deaf ears, as both Mr and Mrs Jones and their three sons just looked at the twins without any sort of acknowledgement. They did not even say goodbye. The twins might just as well not have been there, which is how they had felt for most of the year. Had Hardy Flower and Daisy Thomas been that bad? Perhaps Mrs Jones breathed an inward sigh of relief now that the nosy and meddlesome boy was going home – now she could rut in the fields without fear of him popping up from nowhere like a frightened rabbit. Perhaps Mr Jones worried that his wife would not get as horny now that she wouldn't be watched by the nosy little London brat. And perhaps the eldest Jones boy wanted to find out just that bit more about girls, as did his brothers ... but the Jones family's victims of physical and sexual abuse were going home.

But for how long?

9

Hardy Flower – War Worker

When Daisy and Hardy Flower returned to Gravesend, it seemed to them as if they had never been away. But they had been away, and when they did return home, there was very little welcome for them. The only difference Hardy Flower could see was that the other kids were bigger. As always, the twins went back to school immediately and into the next class up from the one they had left the previous year. Eventually, the twins would have attended no less that seven schools, so that their learning was severely disrupted. The class which they went into at the junior school was the upper class where the children were preparing to take their scholarship exams for the local grammar school. The Thomas twins had no choice but to sit the exam as well, chewing their fingernails and not having a clue as to the answers. Their education, whether they were coming home or going away, was always turned upside down, which meant that very often they were at the bottom of their class.

Later, after the exams, a teacher approached Hardy Flower and asked what he had thought of the exams.

Putting on a brave front, he answered nonchalantly,

'Huh! It was dead easy!'

But her answer was very curt. 'Well then, Hardy Flower Thomas, why didn't you pass, then?'

The bragging kid felt just like the German bombers he had seen hurtling down from the skies – 'Shot down in flames'.

The German air-raids continued on a regular basis, almost every day and night. The English war effort was well under way with everybody 'doing their bit', including the children. Every Saturday morning, a team of three boys and four girls met at the end of Park Road, under the leadership of their 'leading-hand', Leon Tartle. He was the eldest, and because he wore very thick horn-rimned spectacles he was considered to be the 'brains' of the Park Road Salvage Team. Plump and chubby-faced, he lived in a mortgaged and detached house with his parents and wore trousers with, as he boasted, inner linings.

Nearest to him lived the Taylor sisters, who also wore thick-lensed spectacles, which made their unseeing eyes look like pinpoints staring from beneath their untidy black fringes. Their scrawny mother bought second-hand clothes for them, which were pinned together here and there. Mr Taylor, their father and the local odd-job electrician, made suggestive pictures from his magic lantern slides or so it was rumoured. Next door to the Taylors lived Sandra, a pleasant, clean, clever and well-dressed kid who went to the local convent school for girls. For her to attend the 'posh' school, her father worked all the hours under the sun somewhere in Tilbury Docks. So rarely did he put in an appearance in the street that he wasn't very often recognised by the neighbours. Sandra's mother was a tiny Scots lady who was usually spotted by the kids peering through the curtains and was as mad as a hatter. Sandra would eventually make it to university, and become a Bachelor of Science – never to return to her parents or Park Road.

Halfway along the road lived Mr and Mrs Thomas and their children. Cliff, Ken and Jim, the eldest sons, were away in the armed services and made only fleeting visits. Rose, the eldest daughter, was away training to be a nurse, which left Timmy the baby, with the twins, Hardy Flower and his sister Daisy – always referred to as 'the scruffy kids from the poor family'. Just round the corner from Park Road lived Hardy Flower's pal whom everybody called 'Wocco'. These were the seven children who made up the Salvage Team for the area.

Every Saturday morning, the team paraded with their childish pride, under the watchful eye of the sullen and strutting Leon Tartle, who loved to find something wrong. As he was in charge, he insisted on pinning their white armband above their elbow, sometimes blatantly sticking the point of the pin into the team members' arms. The armband had a huge red 'S' painted on it, which was their official insignia, denoting that they were the local 'Salvage Collectors'. Leon Tartle insisted on wearing two armbands, one on each arm, as he was 'in command'.

Once the team had been allotted their areas for salvage collecting, they went in pairs to every house in their road, politely asking: 'Any salvage, please?' Anything they collected was taken to a solitary garage where the air-raid wardens sat drinking tea. Exactly on the dot at noon, Leon would give his orders.

'It is now time for you to go home for your lunch, but be back here at exactly one o'clock!' Hardy Flower was always under the impression that 'lunch' was a sandwich wrapped up in a piece of yesterday's newspaper and carried to wherever you spent your day, while 'dinner' was what you had if you were lucky enough to go home for a meal.

Exactly at one o'clock the collectors reported back to Leon, who always demanded: 'Did you remember to wash your hands before you had your lunch? Hold them out for me to inspect!'

Hardy Flower hadn't been home, let alone had lunch.

'No, I haven't washed my hands, Leon,' the grubby kid answered as he straightened up to attention.

A look of stark horror came over the supercilious leader's face. Then he'd snarl: 'You filthy little swine! You'll get all manner of diseases!'

He spoke with his hands on hips, peering down his nose at Hardy Flower through his horned-rimmed spectacles which were perched on the end of his nose.

Hardy Flower thought to himself, 'I bet he wears underpants!'

Doing the salvage job on Saturdays had its rewards, and of course Hardy Flower always got to the comics first. Once he had read though them, he sold them at school for a penny each – something which he considered to be one of his perks. Any cooking utensils which were not in need of repair were always welcomed by Mrs Flower Thomas, along with anything else which 'might come in useful'.

During the winter months, there was another job which Hardy Flower had to do before the salvage team went on parade. Early on Saturday, with no choice or opportunity to protest, he had to go and collect a bag of coke. The old gasworks, situated adjacent to the local canal basin, always had industrial coke for sale every Saturday morning. The chunks were too large even for industrial use, but, if anybody cared to collect it, it was there for sixpence, for a one-hundredweight bag. Hardy Flower's father always arranged for 'my boy' to borrow a huge old railway barrow. It was upright, with two small iron wheels, and was extremely heavy to push, even without a load, let alone fully loaded. First thing on Saturday morning, Hardy Flower had to go and collect the barrow from a place that lay in the opposite direction from where he had to pick up the coke.

Arriving at the gasworks, Hardy Flower queued up and paid the sixpence, then got on the end of another long queue to wait for a sixpenny-worth load of coke to come hurtling down a chute. As it spilled everywhere, and Hardy flower rushed to load his barrow, the rest of the queue bawled out: 'We haven't got all day! ... Get a move on, you lazy little bleeder!'

Going through the gasworks gate was a downwards incline and Hardy Flower, not being very strong, couldn't quite keep hold of the barrow, which consequently took him and the load of coke down to the jetty railway lines. Often as not, the coke spilled out across the tracks, much to the amusement of the loco engine driver and the crew of the coal barges. Once more, the skinny boy filled up the barrow and started for home again, first over the cobblestones, which made the going harder, and then along the proper road, which made things smoother.

Three hundred yards past the local swimming pool, on to the main road of the town, was a long and tedious trek, followed by a further five hundred yards up Love Lane and past the army barracks, to reach the bottom of Windmill Hill. The through road to Windmill Street was reasonably flat, but the following three hundred yards was the killer for Hardy Flower – by the time he had got to the top of Windmill Street, he was well and truly knackered. At that point, there was an old iron seat, which was a convenient resting place for the undernourished and skinny boy.

The rest of the journey was comparatively easy, as it was all downhill. With sore and blistered hands, Hardy Flower finally trundled the 'giant's' barrow along Park Road, dodging in and out of the bomb damage and debris. He finally dumped the load of coke outside his parents' back door, feeling quite proud of the fact that he had accomplished his mission. Oh how he wanted a drink of water! But immediately on his return, Mrs Flower Thomas's voice always called out:

'Hardy Flower! Your father's gone to work, and he said to tell you to get the barrow back as soon as possible, and when that's done, to break the coke up into little bits – or else you'll feel the back of his hand!' He cringed inwardly, knowing only too well that when his dad left him a message, saying 'Do it, or else!' he had no choice. His heart sank at the thought of just sitting there monotonously hitting the coke with the back of his father's small axe.

Hardy Flower met another lad when he went back to the

old school whom he hadn't known before. His name was Colin Fowler. They got on very well and became very good pals until they left school. Colin Fowler and Hardy Flower had the special something which made them inseparable bosom pals – Colin's pocket money. With it, they'd sometimes buy sausages or sausage meat to take out to the woods. The bigger and rougher Hardy Flower sneaked off with his mum's frying pan, and somehow or other the two boys obtained a box of matches. The two inseparable boys took bread and dripping for frying. Hardy Flower's father's axe was always handy for lopping off the branches of dead trees, and with these they built their woodland camp. Colin and his rough friend, Hardy Flower, invited anybody else who could supply anything to eat to tag along. Their camping area was in some woods known as Painters' Ash.

During the war years lots of kids built camps and cooked their goodies in Painters' Ash. Sometimes they built a treehouse, so they could see whether any other gangs were creeping up on them. The gangs never worried about the weather. If they got wet, they ran about until their clothes were dry. On the odd occasion, their clothes got *too* dry when their campfire ended up engulfing the whole camp. The two pals never went back to the same spot, just in case the local gamekeeper was waiting for the gang.

Colin and Hardy Flower always went to Colin's house to play. Colin lived in a very clean and tidy house, alongside the very select Mid Kent Golf Club. The two boys often played on Colin's dad's neatly cut lawn, where they erected a tent, where the neighbouring kids would come to play with them. Hardy Flower once asked his dad, 'Why can't we have a lawn?' His dad's very curt answer was: 'You can't eat grass, boy!' Hardy Flower had to admit the truth of this. The hungry boy had tried to eat grass, but it had made him sick.

When the weather was dull, Colin's mum allowed the two boys to sit indoors, in front of a coal fire where they read the latest comics, which were actually delivered to the house – a luxury envied by Hardy Flower. It was on a Saturday during mid-summer and halfway through the war, when Colin's mum invited her son's rough-and-ready friend to stay for lunch, which he readily accepted. The sparkling white tablecloth was already laid, and on it stood sparkling cutlery and crockery. That was good enough for Hardy Flower, who jumped up on to a chair and sat holding his knife and fork pointing upwards and ready to eat, just like his dad did.

Colin went into the kitchen and Mrs Fowler said: 'Hardy Flower, dear, would you like to wash your hands before you eat?'

'What a funny question to ask?' the young and innocent boy thought as he looked up at her. But he knew he had to say something. If he wasn't polite, it would get back to his mum, who he was sure was looking for a good excuse to lay the washing cudgel across his back again.

'No thank you, Mrs Fowler!'

His friend's mum looked taken aback. He could hear his friend Colin scrubbing his hands at the kitchen sink, and Hardy Flower still wondered why.

At the table Hardy Flower was determined to do the right thing – to wipe his knife clean with his tongue, and wave it about as he talked with his mouth full … he was sure his manners were impeccable. When Hardy Flower had finished lunch by wiping a crust of bread round his plate, the sprightly Mrs Fowler asked him whether he would like to go on a picnic the next day, as she and some friends were taking their children to Wombwell Park, which was close by.

'There is no need to bring anything, Hardy Flower dear. Do tell mummy. We have everything we need, and everything is arranged.'

The next day was a Sunday, and Hardy Flower's mum agreed to let him go on the picnic.

'Yes, you can go, but you'll take your own picnic.'

Mrs Flower Thomas had her pride, and, after all, food was rationed and people do talk. Hardy Flower was overjoyed and couldn't wait for the afternoon to come round.

'There you are, then!' Mrs Flower Thomas handed her son his 'picnic-pack'.

'Off you go and behave yourself – or else!'

Hardy Flower was all ready for the special day out. His hair was smarmed down with soap lather, and, although he had wet the bed as usual the night before, his shirt had dried against his warm stomach. It was a bit 'niffy', but he was used to it. Everything seemed OK and Hardy Flower felt smarter and smarmier than the school sneak.

The 'happy to be one of the nice kids' picnic-pack consisted of a bottle of water and four sandwiches made from stale bread and dripping fat. The doorstep-thick sandwiches were wrapped in a piece of newspaper, and put into an empty 'National Dried Milk' box, which baby Tim had finished with. That Sunday was a lovely summer's day, and as soon as the twins had completed the greasy washing-up in the usual cold water, Hardy Flower was off to Colin's house, where all the other kids and their mums were waiting and ready to go, dressed in summer light-weight clothes and all shining like new pins.

The bus came along and everybody clambered on to it, all shouting and singing, except Hardy Flower, that is, who didn't have any money. Not a word had been said about bus fares, but, then, hadn't Colin's mum said, 'Don't bring anything?' However, Mrs Fowler was a kindly young mum, and as she had invited him, she kept her eyes on Hardy Flower and paid for his bus fare.

Twenty minutes later, into Wombwell Park they all ran, anxious to get on to the swings and roundabouts, especially Hardy Flower, who shyly approached Mrs Fowler. 'Mrs Fowler, here's my share of the picnic,' he said, then proudly handed the pleasant young mum his bottle of water and the well-wrapped 'dripping' sandwiches, which no doubt were covered with dried-milk powder.

The very sympathetic mum, Mrs Fowler, started to say something as she opened the box, but as she was about to speak, there came a mighty roar, and when they looked up there above the children's playground flew a huge German bomber, right overhead. It flew so low that everybody could see the pilot's head above the frightening black cross insignia of the German Luftwaffe on the fuselage and wings. On the tail of the aircraft was the dreaded black swastika. Everybody was frightened, and even more so, when they heard the 'rata-tat-tat', of a machine gun being fired. Nobody seemed to know whether it was the pilot shooting at them, or some local soldiers shooting at the airplane.

The German airplane disappeared, and the children carried on playing until it was teatime. All the mums called their kids over to the huge picnic cloth, but there was no sign of Hardy Flower's bread and dripping or his bottle of water. Hardy Flower was handed some cakes and tiny sandwiches, with a glass of lemonade, which he really got stuck into. 'I bet they've kept my sandwiches and water for themselves,' he thought indignantly. The puzzled boy eventually got them, but when he handed them round politely, nobody wanted them, so he ate them himself. There was milk powder on the edges of the crusts, and Hardy Flower thought that salt and pepper might have been a much tastier addition.

After the picnic, everybody had another run-around, with more turns on the swings and roundabouts, then suddenly it was time for the picnickers to catch the bus and go home. Once more, Hardy Flower's friend's mum, Mrs Fowler, paid his fare home. He had really enjoyed himself on the picnic and, by the time he arrived home, it was time for bed. Hardy Flower went to bed in his day clothes, which were also his pyjamas. He was not due for a wash – not just yet.

Every man and boy had their hair cut regularly once a

week, and it was always a 'short back and sides'. There was
no such thing as fashions and styles for men. It was straight
up the back and sides, with an electric clipper. Every barber's
shop was always packed out, with men sitting or standing,
miserably waiting their turn. Hardy Flower hated having to
wait for over an hour to have his hair clipped. Most of all,
he hated the way most of the clippered hair went down his
back underneath his shirt, where it stayed until the next bath
night.

Mr Hardy Thomas, was on the 'two-till-ten' afternoon and
evening shift at the factory where he worked, and one midweek
morning he went for his haircut. The barber got busy with
the shears but, as usual, there was an air-raid, and the anti-
aircraft guns began to fire, which was too much for the
barber. He put the clippers down and ripped off his apron,
saying to Hardy Thomas: 'I'm off! Come back when the raid
is over.'

Off he went, running along the road to his own air-raid
shelter. Hardy Flower's dad struggled out from under the
sheet cover, and he too ran home. Unfortunately, he had to
go to work before the air-raid was over, with one half of his
head clippered, and one half hairy, and the story was that
he'd also had half of his moustache cut off. It took many
weeks for Mr Hardy Thomas to live the embarrassment down,
after his 'h'air-raid'.

Mr Hardy Thomas often caused a few laughs, despite being
a strict father. Another humorous occasion was when he was
on the 'six-till-two' shift when the family had been in the
air-raid shelter all night and things were very dodgy with the
exceptionally heavy bombing, aimed once more at the munition
factories on the River Thames, at Gravesend and Northfleet.
The deafening noise of the bombs whistling down and exploding
had kept everybody awake throughout the night, in what
they called their 'iron grave'. Buildings could be seen burning
in all directions. The sky was quite lit up in an orange haze,

with smoke drifting about like a dense fog. Suddenly, there was a huge explosion and an even bigger fire could be seen reflected in the sky over the rooftops. The Tilbury Hotel had been hit by a bomb, and would be burned to the ground by midday. The explosion was so loud that Mr Hardy Thomas shouted.

'Oh my good Gawd! That's the bloody house coming down. I'll go and have a look.'

At that particular time of the morning, the only light to see by was the aerial searchlights and fires from the nearby explosions. As he climbed out of the shelter, Hardy Thomas pulled the sack covering to one side. Unfortunately for him the house brick which held the old sack in position fell on top of his head.

'Oh, my giddy godfathers! What next?' Then he swore.

He swore in a long-drawn-out, self-pitying voice, which the family all found extremely amusing. Mr Hardy Thomas stumbled up the garden path, to try and see what had happened, and when he returned, he shouted into the air-raid shelter.

'The house is still standing. You lot stay in there. I'm off to work, or else I'll be late.'

Mr Hardy Thomas had to walk the two-and-a-half miles to work. During the forty-four years he worked for the old W.T. Henley, he was late for work only twice.

Mr Hardy Thomas bought himself a pushbike to cycle to work on, but luck was not on his side. Cycling to work for the early shift in the blackout, he collided with another cyclist going down the hill into Windmill Street, where he fell and broke his arm. That was the end of Mr Hardy Thomas having a pushbike. Working-class people couldn't afford cars in those days, while most tradesman made their deliveries by horse and cart or push-carts. It was only doctors and professional people who could afford to ride in a car.

During the war years, the blackout meant exactly that –

absolutely no lights to be seen during the hours of darkness. All vehicles had to have the lenses of their lamps blackened with paint. On Saturday evenings, parents went to do their late-night shopping, which, in those days, was only available in the old marketplace. The poorer and hard-up people went there to try and get some end-of-day bargains. At Christmas-time everything had to go, and on those occasions there was a lot of humour and backchat, because people had time for each other. On one of those Saturday evenings, Mr Hardy Thomas went alone, to pick up some bargains in the meat market, and, along with the weekend joint, he bought a string of sausages. Then, once he'd made the necessary purchases, he decided that it was time for him to go for a quick pint, which, in turn, led to another and meeting up with some workmates. Obviously, he ended up quite tipsy when the pubs turned out, at ten o'clock. When the final bell rang, Mr Hardy Thomas decided to walk up and over Windmill Hill.

On top of Windmill Hill there had once stood a village, all of whose buildings had been made of timber. However, in 1899 there had been a big outdoor party to celebrate the 'Relief of Mafekin' in the Boer War, in South Africa. The celebratory bonfire had got out of hand, resulting in the whole village being burned to the ground, simply because some local youths had vandalised the fire hoses from the town. And so, forty years later, all that remained of the village was the pit where the windmill's millstones had lain, and it was into that same pit that Mr Hardy Thomas tumbled, in his carefree and boozy state. The more he tried to scramble up the sandy side of the pit, the more he slipped backwards into the bottom. Hardy Thomas finally gave up and fell asleep. And as he slept, a full moon came up over the estuary of the River Thames, making the distant waves shimmer and the sky bright. The brightness, of course, woke the tiddly man up in the early hours of the morning, and, much to his dismay, the Sunday joint had disappeared, and, to his wrath, a stray dog was finishing off his 'string' of sausages. From that night on, Mr Hardy Thomas swore to his dying day that there had been two moons shining down on him that night.

During 1943 Hardy Flower donned his first uniform, to become a 'Wolf Cub'. It seemed at the time, to be the 'in' thing for a ten-year-old boy to become a 'Wolf Cub'. The starting age was eight, but the skinny kid was always a slow-starter and he eventually joined the Wolf Cub pack when he was ten years old. Of course, the school sneaks and the namby-pambies had the proper soft green woollen jerseys, with bright blue-and-gold scarves round their necks, the colours of the St Mary's 11th Gravesend Cub Pack. The Cubs preferred to call the scarf by its proper name – 'neckerchief'. It must be apparent to the reader that there were a lot of 'school sneaks' in the world of Hardy Flower. Anybody who was cleaner and more privileged than he was, was, in his opinion, a 'school sneak'. 'They' had polished shoes, while Hardy Flower had hobnailed boots or sandals, depending on the time of year. 'Their' socks were knee-length and diamond-patterned on the turnover. But Hardy Flower was strong and brave because his mum had said 'You don't need socks! They're cissy!'

'Their' trousers were pressed and held up with a coloured elastic belt with a 'snake' clasp. On top of their heads, and supported by their ears, they wore the green, gold-piped Cub's cap. One good spin, and the kid would go round, and his cap would stay still. The 'posher' the kid and the cleaner he looked, the more badges and 'Sixer' stripes he would have. The 'Sixer' was a Cub Corporal, who led a patrol of six Cubs; the Sixer's next step up would be as a 'Senior Sixer'. And so Hardy Flower became a Cub, and for a few weeks he belonged to the 'plainclothes' branch. There was no chance of him going to the Cubs' stores to purchase his uniform, because, even if he had been given the money to buy it, he would probably have bought cakes and pies with it instead.

Hardy Flower was a patient boy, owing to always having had to wait for almost everything. A friend of a neighbour told his mum, Mrs Flower Thomas, about a second-hand Cub uniform, which hadn't been used for quite some time, and was for sale. The opportunity was taken and the jersey, cap and neckerchiefs were purchased, straight from the ragbag, complete with a broken 'woggle' – 'It can be mended and the uniform washed!' That was Mrs Flower Thomas's stern assumption.

On the next Cub night, the new Wolf Cub donned his uniform, ready to go on parade in full regalia as a fully-fledged member of Saint Mary's 11th Gravesend Cub Pack. There, Hardy Flower was on parade, wearing the filthy jersey, crumpled neckerchief and an old pair of Territorial Army training shorts, which would probably have disappeared if rubbed against a bar of soap. The tall and skinny but very proud boy wore no cap and no socks, but Hardy Flower was on parade with a uniform, and so very, very proud!

The Wolf Cub headquarters was a very old and derelict railway carriage, which stood adjacent to St Mary's Sunday School, at the edge of Woodlands Park. Hardy Flower learned his knots and first aid, and how to light a fire – his previous way had been with a box of matches and a gallon of paraffin; the Cubs' way was with a pile of old newspapers and a box of matches. In the pack, he was referred to as 'The Lone Wolf'. Hardy Flower stayed with the Wolf Cubs until he went on another 'trip' a year later. 'The Lone Wolf' never became a 'Sixer' or earned any badges of distinction.

Opposite the Wolf Cubs' headquarters stood several large houses, each surrounded by its own grounds. All of them had been taken over for the duration of the war as billets for the soldiers, and the only badge which Hardy Flower went after was on a hat which a soldier had dropped in Woodlands Park. As soon as he dropped it, Hardy Flower was there, grabbing for the bright and shiny brass badge, then he was up and away. The soldier had been teasing the kids, so Hardy Flower thought he would teach the soldier a lesson.

'A nice shiny soldier's badge; just what I want!' Hardy Flower thought, as he made the snatch. Then, much to his dismay, something big, thick, strong and hairy grabbed at him.

Snatching at his hat, the soldier snarled: 'You little bastard!'

Like an eel, Hardy Flower twisted free, and he was off. There was no reason for him to stay there and get a good hiding; he could get those any time, at home.

During his short spell as a Wolf Cub, there was one little incident which Hardy Flower took advantage of, which was the 'Bob-a-Job Week'. This involved the Scouts and Wolf Cubs donning their uniforms, and each of them going to an allotted amount of houses in his own road, to offer his services and do a job for a 'bob' – five new pennies. Any task was undertaken for the 'bob', such as cleaning windows or polishing shoes, chopping wood, or tidying up the garden. All proceeds went into the Cubs and Scouts Fund.

Hardy Flower worked with great fervour, and near the end of his work day, he felt very tired, but he had one more house to do, so in he went and hammered on the door. It was opened by an old man.

'Now then, young man!' the man growled softly, 'Are you trying to knock the Lord Jesus down out of heaven with all that noise?'

'Please, Sir,' Hardy Flower snivelled, 'it's Bob-a-Job-week. Have you any jobs?'

It so happened that the old boy wanted his hedge trimming, which Hardy Flower did with gusto, thinking that he was clipping off the ears of all the school sneaks he had ever known. After the hedge-trimming, the kindly old gent thought he would like a flowerbed weeded and seeded, but by now it was time for Hardy Flower to report back to the Cub

Master, with his 'bobs for the jobs'. Before he left, Hardy Flower suggested to the old boy that, if he wanted flowers planted, Hardy Flower would have to put the seeds in the following Saturday. To this the gentleman agreed.

The next week Hardy Flower was up bright and early, hell-bent on becoming a gardener. Before he left home, he paid a visit to the old wash-house-cum-shed-cum-junk-hole. That dirty old building might be full of junk, but Hardy Flower knew exactly where every little thing was kept or even hidden. Minutes later, he went to his garden job with two packets of his dad's flower seeds and got started on his labours. The kind old gentleman came out with cake and lemonade and asked the 'gardener' how much the seeds had cost. The packets were marked at threepence. He went into the house and minutes later he returned with a one-shilling piece and a sixpence piece. Smiling serenely, he spoke to Hardy Flower.

'Here's sixpence for the seeds, and a shilling for your Bob-a-Job.'

The kindly old gent was under the impression that 'Bob-a-Job Week' was a permanent thing, and the rascal that Hardy Flower was he let the old boy carry on thinking it, as he continually found jobs which he suggested he could do next week. The kindly and trusting man allowed Hardy Flower to be his gardener for three weeks, after which the old boy realised that he had been conned by the skinny boy from over the road and made the entrepreneurial Wolf Cub redundant. But Hardy Flower enjoyed the cakes and lemonade which he bought with the one-shilling piece.

Next door to the house where the entrepreneurial Cub had been the 'gardener' lived the Salvage Team boss Leon Tartle. Daisy Thomas always seemed to have a crush on the school sneak who wore thick-rimmed spectacles, and very often she would leave a note in the fork of a tree for 'Dear Leon', enclosing one square of chocolate.

A new pirate film called *The Black Swan* was being shown

at the local cinema, known as the 'flea-pit' because it was the cheapest cinema in town. Hardy Flower dearly wanted to go and see the swashbuckling and swordsmanship of the pirates, but he had no money, until he found an old Indian shilling with the King's head on it. Now this king was wearing a crown, while English coins were minus the crown. It wasn't legal tender, but this did not stop Hardy Flower who did a fast dash up to the flea-pit's cashier's box and handed over the coin while carefully covering the king's crown with his finger. The cashier gave him his change and Hardy Flower could hardly disguise his glee – more cakes and pies for him when the film was over.

Daisy's and Hardy Flower's pocket money was sixpence a week, if their dad was in a good mood, but to earn it they had to run all the errands. Also, the boy had to help his dad on his two allotments and in his garden. Both of the allotments were a mile away, which Hardy Flower had to walk. Most of the jobs were either weeding or carrying watering cans backward and forwards between the water taps and the gardens, and Hardy Flower was always tired before he started.

The 'decider' for collecting their sixpence was on the Sunday afternoon, when the family had finished dinner. Mr Hardy Thomas would go to bed and sleep his beer off, and everybody else would disappear. Mrs Flower Thomas always disappeared upstairs, too, taking with her the *News of the World* for her husband. The twins' elder brother and sister always went out with their friends, which meant that Daisy and Hardy Flower were left to do the after-dinner washing up.

Mrs Flower Thomas always used every cooking utensil in the kitchen, which made the washing-up a real chore. The cooker was always messy and greasy, the saucepans somehow had burnt vegetables stuck to the insides, and there was no such thing as washing-up liquid. All that the twins could use was a piece of old towel, a heavy scouring wire and lots of 'elbow grease'. If the twins were lucky, they would get two kettles of hot water, then, when they had finished the washing and drying-up, they got their sixpence 'wages'. Before his dad went to the pub on Sundays, Hardy Flower had to clean and polish his shoes. Mr Hardy Thomas was an 'old soldier', and always expected the black leather to be sparkling.

Daisy and Hardy Flower had to go to Sunday school in the morning, though they knew it was just to get them out of the way. Hardy Flower could think of at least four much nicer Sunday schools quite near to their home where he and his sister Daisy could have enjoyed going. But for some reason, somebody had told the twins' parents that the Congregation Church had a good Sunday school, and, it was also where their parents had been married in 1920 and where the twins had been christened.

Unfortunately for the twins, there was a family of four girls and two boys who also went to the same Sunday school, and they too could have gone to a Sunday school much nearer to their own home. The unfortunate part for the twins was that the family made up a gang of six 'heavies', all of whom were extremely well built and never to be reckoned with. It was amazing how big they all were, especially as they were living on wartime rations. For some unknown reason the heavy kids didn't like Daisy and Hardy Flower, and they showed it with a bit of pushing and shoving, along with threats, all of which made the twins' Sunday mornings quite unpleasant.

The Sunday school class always assembled in the basement of the church, and it was always at the base of the steps where the overfed kids waited for the twins – once they were trapped at the bottom of the steps, there was no way out. A very tall, lean man with a hooked nose shepherded the children into a huge dark room in the basement, to be taught their scriptures, or, terrified out of their skins as they listened to old Hook Nose's stories of doom. When Sunday school was finished, the big kids chased the lightly-built twins, who had no choice but to run, and whichever way they went, the bigger kids followed. There were three choices of route for the bully-boys and girls to take to go home, and two of those were the same as those that Daisy and Hardy Flower could take. So, every week, Sunday school for the twins was a hell of harassment, so much so that eventually they played truant from the dark Gothic-looking church. Instead of going to the church, they sat on Windmill Hill, which overlooked the church, and listened to a brass band, until they saw the kids coming out of the church – then they knew it was time to scarper and go home.

There were several things that Hardy Flower's mum used to do which puzzled him. The fact that they didn't have a bathroom, or a decent place to wash, or even hot water, or indeed much living space, left much to be desired. However, when their new baby brother had his nappy changed, he always had his face wiped over with the wet nappy. So, of course, Hardy Flower asked why. Not all babies had a bath every day, did they? His mother's answer was that the wet nappy would give the baby rosy cheeks. Being ten years old, Hardy Flower accepted the explanation.

Later that same year he watched while his baby brother had his bath, and afterwards, into the same water, went two days of dinner crockery, to be washed. There were many things which Hardy Flower had his doubts about, things that puzzled him, but he was just a young boy, unable to comprehend the whys and wherefores. Then he'd run off, his retentive mind storing up the questions, to be answered at a later date. Another regular happening – whether or not it was the custom or the done thing, he didn't know – was the sight of buckets or bowls of water into which his mother put tightly screwed-up cloths to soak. That was OK, Hardy Flower thought, because lots of washing was put in to soak, but the outsides of those buckets and bowls were always blood-stained. The stains started at the top and ran down in dribbles. Hardy Flower very often felt sick when he saw this, and felt disturbed. He knew something had to be wrong, especially with children running about. But, then, the ten-year-old was just a young know-nothing brat.

10

From Cudgel to Carving Knife and Frying Pan

The third year of the Second World War was not only the halfway mark of the conflict. It was also the turning point where the British started to turn the tide and win some battles, which meant that a high percentage of the armed services were on immediate standby. It also meant that the young servicemen were out to enjoy life – while they had the chance.

At that time 'teenager' was not yet a known status – children of that age were referred to as 'young ladies' or 'young men'. That's not to say that the young girls and boys didn't have fun. Hardy Flower's sister Rose was seventeen and had already had various boyfriends. On several occasions, Rose had gone out with an army friend of their brother, Jimmy. Very suddenly, that friend was sent abroad, to 'do his bit', much to Mrs Flower Thomas's regret. Mrs Flower Thomas thought the handsome soldier would be the ideal partner for her daughter Rose. Rose herself thought he was a wimp, and was pleased to see him go. Then, along came a Royal Air Force 'Brylcreem boy', a poser whom Rose thought she was in love with, much to her mum's regret.

'What's this one's name then?' asked her father, and when Rose answered 'Peter, Dad,' he immediately came back with, 'And I suppose the next bugger will be bloody Paul!'

Like millions of other girl–boy relationships, the front garden wall was the lounging place for Rose and her current boyfriend, Peter. But they had yet to be accepted by Rose's mum, Mrs Flower Thomas, who seemed to have something nagging at the back of her mind. Perhaps it was her own very brief courtship, or the fact that she didn't like the smarmy creep who was 'chatting up' her daughter at the front gate. What would the neighbours think?

Several times during the late evening Mrs Flower Thomas told her daughter: 'It's time you were in!' But Mrs Flower Thomas got little or no response from her daughter and it was then that Mrs Flower Thomas 'flipped her lid'. Hardy Flower had sneaked into his mum and dad's front bedroom to peer round the curtained windows at what Rose and her Peter were up to – but at the sound of his mum's raised voice he did a quick return downstairs, by sliding down the bannister. At the same time, his mum rushed past him and through the narrow hallway to the front door. In one hand she carried the cast-iron frying pan, and in her other was a huge bone-handled carving knife. Mrs Flower Thomas was on the warpath, hotly pursued by her twins, Daisy and Hardy Flower, screaming their young lungs out. If the front door hadn't been open, their irate mum would have gone straight through it, as solid as it was. There was a lot of strong language, such as 'bugger' and 'bloody', bandied about. Then came the clang as Peter the airman's head came into contact with the cast-iron frying pan. Behind the twins came more pursuers, their dad and two brothers, Ken and Jimmy, who were on weekend leave. All three had got to grips with Mrs Flower Thomas, but not before Rose's thumb was accidentally sliced open with the carving knife. Rose ran in screaming.

'I'm cut! I'm cut! I'm dying! I'm dying!'

She held her thumb high above her head and it was pouring with blood as she fled into the small room at the back of the house. There she promptly fainted. By now Mrs Flower Thomas had quietened down, and the cut thumb and faint brought out all of Mrs Flower Thomas's nursing instincts. But not before Hardy Flower got his ear belted, just for being there, and was very curtly told to 'Clear off!'

There was nothing for the skinny nine-year-old kid to do except rake around the streets. There was nothing to do indoors either, no TV, no comics or books, though Mr Hardy Thomas did have a two-band radio, with serious discussions on one side, and music, typically played by the Palm Court Orchestra, on the other. Hardy Flower couldn't stay in the kitchen either – it was only big enough for one adult to stand in front of the sink or at the grimy and fat-splashed gas stove, and the other rooms downstairs had the 'grown-ups' in them, arguing about who was doing what. Once again, the adventurous kid sat on the bedroom windowsill, daring himself to do his first parachute drop with his paper parachute hooked on to the collar of his woollen jersey.

Post-menstrual tension was not yet medically established, other than for a woman who was thought to be 'going off her trolley', and it possibly played a big part in some of the household happenings of the Thomas family in the 1940s. Over this time Hardy Flower became aware that his mum suffered some traumatic experiences which he could never understand. There were many late nights when Mrs Flower Thomas attacked her daughter Rose for staying out late, and had to be dragged off and away from the unfortunate girl. 'Late night' was considered to be after nine o'clock.

During the summer term Hardy Flower's class was to have weekly swimming lessons at the swimming pool and the children were instructed to bring their swimming trunks and a towel to school. When the exciting day arrived, Hardy Flower didn't have any trunks, so he mentioned it to his mum, hoping she would offer to buy him a pair like the other boys wore, but as usual Mrs Flower Thomas's reply was sharp and commanding.

'Well? If you need swimming trunks, you can make some!

Go and find your old pullover, the one without sleeves!'

After he'd dug it out from some dark and damp corner, the boy had to search for a needle and sock-mending wool, then he spent a half-hour sewing up the V-neck with a blanket stitch.

The enthusiastic boy did as he was told, then his mum looked at it, saying, 'Put your legs through the arm holes, and tie a piece of string round your waist, and that'll do! Off you go!'

And off to the pool the kids went, most of them wearing summer sandals and white ankle socks with their soft summer clothes. Under their arm they carried a neatly rolled-up towel, with their coloured swimwear inside it. Although Hardy Flower didn't have any socks on, he still wore his boots with the studs in the soles, and of course the usual 'wet-the-bed shirt' tucked into his trousers. Under his arm he carried the remnant of an old towel, with the sewn-up upside-down pullover, complete with a piece of hairy garden string. The towel had a large hole in it, but no matter. The schoolchildren had lots of fun in the open-air pool – they were used to seeing the twins in their years-old hand-me-downs, so Hardy Flower's makeshift trunks hardly fazed them at all. Until he was fifteen years old Hardy Flower could only swim by doing the 'dog paddle'. (He would improve.)

Football was the next sport which Hardy Flower became interested in, so he asked for a pair of football boots, and a football for his birthday. Yes, Hardy Flower could have what he asked for, *if* he behaved himself!

On his tenth birthday, the exuberant birthday boy was up bright and early and full of excitement at the thought of getting some new football gear. There was no fancy wrapping for the twins in those days, but at the end of his bed, and much to his disappointment, was an old pair of discarded football boots, and a worn-out old football which had the appearance and shape of a rugby ball. The leather panels were the shape of orange segments, and the stitches were broken at the seams. It was so old, in shape and design, that it probably dated to circa 1890.

The air-raids continued, and everybody had to 'duck and dive' into the air-raid shelters. Very often there would be harassed mums with their babes in arms or prams, dragging two or three yowling toddlers down into the underground shelters. Sometimes Daisy and Hardy Flower would sit and play in the air-raid shelter in the garden, the 'dungeon' of Hardy Flower's 'castle'. If there wasn't an air-raid going on, Daisy might bring several schoolfriends home to play, and Hardy Flower, being an extrovert in the making, would always get among them to show off.

In the air-raid shelter there was always the comfort of a candle and a box of matches. Acting the man, the grubby, piss-stained kid started bragging about how grown up he was, and that he smoked. The extrovert boy's bragging got him the response he wanted – the girls immediately wanted him to *prove* just how grown up he was. Now Hardy Flower had already picked a nice-looking honeysuckle twig and this he now stuck in the corner of his mouth trying to look tough, just like an American gangster in the films. To act out the part, he lit the stub of the candle then quite nonchalantly put the candle flame to the end of his 'cheroot', and went through the film star routine of lighting up. Suddenly he felt as if somebody had put a shovelful of hot coals down his throat as he coughed and spluttered, nearly choking himself to death. He dropped the candle, grabbed the girls' tea-set jug, and swallowed the water inside it to quench his burning throat. Of course, the girls were in hysterics, but almost immediately one of them shouted:

'Look? The candle has fallen over, and it's still alight! We'll all catch fire! Help! ... Help! ... Help!'

There was no real danger, but Hardy Flower still had to act the hero.

'Stand back! I'll see to it; it could be highly dangerous,' he cried, quoting from one of his old comics.

Stepping forwards, the young hero tipped the jug's remaining contents over the candle, which caused the hot melted wax to hiss and crackle loudly. This frightened the smelly show-off brat almost out of his pissy-smelling trousers, and once again the look on his face had the girls crying with laughter.

'That's it!' Hardy Flower thought. 'I'm ten, and there's only one thing to do, with girls like these!'

He grabbed one of the girls and kissed her full on the lips, and immediately the girls stopped laughing. The girl Hardy Flower had kissed took a deep breath and gasped.

'Harrrdee Flow'werr! Hardy Flow'wer!'

The little girl, suddenly in love, was blushing to the roots of her hair. Although there were lots of 'oohs! and aahs!' the other girls put their noses in the air, hoping that he'd kiss them, too. Of course, after the kissing game, the inevitable happened: skinny pissy-pants and the little girl with thick double-glazed spectacles were branded as 'sweethearts'. The 'romance' didn't last very long. His supposed 'sweetheart' told her mum that 'she thought that Hardy Flower was a wretched and smelly boy.

On one of his brother Clifford's flying visits, it was decided that, as only Cliff, Hardy Flower and their mum were there, they would have cream cakes and doughnuts with their tea. Naturally, it fell to the kid of the family to go to the cake shop, for 'sixpenny-worth'. His big brother Cliff, always a true gentleman, only wanted one, and so did their mum for the time being. Hardy Flower would also have one, so, by his calculations, there would be three cream doughnuts left, and as he had run to the shop to get them, they were rightfully his. While his mum and Cliff were talking, Hardy Flower hid the remaining cakes, but Mrs Flower Thomas knew her young son, Hardy Flower, better than he knew himself. An hour later, having seen her soldier son, Cliff, off at the front door, she returned and immediately hauled her brat son out from under the table by his ear.

'Right! Where are they?'

Cream doughnuts were one of Mrs Flower Thomas's favourite treats, along with walnut chocolate creams, which Hardy Flower very often found in his mum's dressing-table drawer, next to a long rubber tube with a big bulb in the centre and a jet nozzle on one end. As he chewed happily on one of his mum's secret walnut creams, he would use the bulbous douche to swipe at and cosh everything in sight, thinking that it was his dad's secret rubber truncheon in case the Germans came.

Now standing on his tiptoes and suspended by one ear, Hardy Flower rapidly owned up as to where he had hidden the cream doughnuts – otherwise, he knew, he'd get a 'clip' round the other ear! He received one of each eventually, another doughnut and a 'clip' round his good ear for hiding the cream cakes.

Rose had ditched her 'Brylcreem boy' in favour of getting in with some friends who had an American soldier staying with them. During the war, there was very little in the way of toys for children. Eventually the American soldier gave Rose a box of marbles, for her to take home for Daisy and Hardy Flower to share. Later, the marbles got mixed together, which meant that the twins had to play together – or quarrel.

Daisy had a huge straw-stuffed rag doll, which was always on her bed. That Daisy loved her doll did not stop it suffering a dreadful demise. Her twin brother had made a camp under her bed and didn't like any foreign infiltrators in or on top of his camp – 'They might be German spies!' He decided there and then that his sister and her ragdoll would have to be bombed immediately! So, out came his marbles to use as bombs, and he made Daisy hold her hands palm downwards on the bed, while he bombed the back of her knuckles from as high as he could reach with imaginary high-explosive marble bombs. Daisy cried so much that, in her temper, she punched and kicked her doll until the straw stuffing poked out of its painted face. Suddenly Hardy Flower felt sorry for the old ragdoll and began to cry, too. But then, to get his own back on Daisy, he wrenched the ragdoll's head off and tore the straw stuffing from its throat. Later, the kid with three sixes on his head played football with the cloth doll's head, and who better to be the goalkeeper than his sister Daisy?

'Any gum, chum?' This became a very familiar refrain when the 'Yanks' came into the war, from both kids and adults alike. In England, sweets were on ration, but the American forces had their sweets issued. Some of the soldiers gave it to the children quite freely, especially if it helped the Yanks 'date' the kids' elder sisters.

Gravesend, a very old and quaint, 'shrimps and winkles' seaside town, had lots of alleys and old backstreets, which Hardy Flower liked to explore on his own. The shrimp, winkles and cockle catchers who sailed out of Bawley Bay wore either a cloth cap and a muffler, or a trilby hat with a collar and tie, which was the fashion. The women wore hats or turbans, especially if they worked in the munition factories.

Most of the streets were two-way traffic, with the exception of High Street, Princes Street, Stone Street and Queen Street. The young loner, Hardy Flower, loved to stand at the bottom of Windmill Street and watch all the double-decked buses going up and down New Road, turning into the various roads which led out of town. Very often, he went to the old town pier, to stand and gaze at the many huge liners, with their various coloured funnels belching out the thick black smoke, as they sailed up and down the River Thames. The liners' decks were always thronged with passengers going abroad. The biggest spectacle was the massive ships of the Orient Line, which sailed to Australia and New Zealand, a voyage which took over six weeks and cost each emigrant £10.

They sailed on ships with names like *Himalaya*, *Orcades* and *Orion*. Up and down the River Thames there were many, many ships of the various shipping lines, carrying both passengers and cargo. There were lots of 'hoots and toots' as the ships let off steam, as they sailed away. For the departing, Gravesend was the last English town that they would ever see as they sailed into the Thames Estuary, on their voyage to Down Under.

After his excursions in and around the town, the scruffy kid always ended up standing at the bottom of Windmill Street, as always, tired and hungry. He became so hungry at times that he started to beg for halfpennies with a pitiful and tear-strained face, saying, 'I've lost my mum's change and she'll belt me with her copper-stick cudgel ... Could you lend me a ha'penny, please? ... Mister!'

They'd look at Hardy Flower's gaunt and grimy face questioningly, and most of them would give him the halfpenny. Hardy Flower the brat would beg for halfpennies and pennies until he had enough money to buy cakes and pies, or fish and chips and to pay his bus fare home. By law the skinny and grimy brat could have been taken into care and charged with begging in the town centre, which was a crime. It would have been 'God help the boy!' if his father had ever found out.

At the time he was begging, Hardy Flower's elder brother Jimmy was medically discharged from the army, due to perforated eardrums, caused by the explosions of the heavy field guns. Jimmy Thomas was employed as a stevedore in Tilbury Docks and soon found out that it meant perks for the dockers if a food container was damaged while being unloaded and it spilt contents within easy reach of the hungry workers, who, in turn, thought about their hungry families at home.

Very often, Jimmy Thomas would come home early from work and straight away he'd light the gas cooker in a very business-like manner. Then he'd bring out his edible 'swag' which he had concealed in various places under his work clothes. It wasn't very often that Hardy Flower got to smell a complete 'full English' at home. Like a latterday Oliver Twist he stood there, mouth wide open, gazing in wonderment at his brother Jimmy's piled-up 'fry-up'. The boy's mouth watered and it seemed to Hardy Flower that his big brother was eating two months' rations in that one luxurious breakfast.

Jimmy carried his loaded tin tea tray in both hands, with his back to his young brother as he went to sit down in a deep armchair and gorge himself silly.

'Gis'a chip, Jimmy? Please!'

Very suddenly Jimmy turned, and the startled kid's eyes opened wide in fright wishing he'd kept his mouth shut. It seemed as if Jimmy Thomas had gone into a silent rage, wanting to vent his anger on his ten-year-old brother Hardy Flower for even daring to speak. The young boy's natural instinct was to do a quick 'runner' because he'd felt the back of Jimmy's huge hand too many times. Then, to his utter amazement, Jimmy thrust the tray of food at Hardy Flower.

'Here! Eat the bloody lot!'

For a second the frightened kid was sure that he was about to be buried beneath a pile of sausages and chips – such was Jimmy's temper, though, according to other older siblings, it was all because of the war.

The very heavy tray was almost too much for Hardy Flower to carry, but he managed it, as his brother Jimmy stormed off in a rage.

As Jimmy Thomas grew older, his 'moods' became a mental burden, but, when progress brought forth some wondrous drugs, he became the most placid and gentle man in the family. Jimmy would be married to a very understanding young lady, though the couple would be bereft of children. As he became older, the drugs became less effective, until one day during a deep and black depression Jimmy tied a stocking round his wife's neck and left her on the floor unconscious. Then he calmly walked into the nearest police station to tell them what he had done. The unfortunate schizophrenic went into hospital and after two years was discharged, walking straight back into the loving arms of his devoted wife. Jimmy Thomas would be destined to suffer his depressive illness for a further thirty-five years until he died of cancer well into his seventies, and all that time his wife would be constantly at his side. Jimmy Thomas was the most handsome man in the Thomas family.

11

1944, Dodging the Doodlebugs

By the spring of 1944 Hardy Flower's brothers had all taken their girlfriends home at some time or other, to meet their mum – Mrs Flower Thomas. Her eldest son, Cliff, had become engaged to one girl, and then, suddenly, through a romantic misunderstanding, the engagement was called off. Then Cliff met another young lady whom he fell in love with, eventually inviting her to come home and meet his family. But it wasn't to be Cliff Thomas's lucky weekend, because both his lady loves turned up at the same time. Unfortunately for Cliff, they were both under the impression that they would marry him.

Being such a young and innocent boy, Hardy Flower was always shooed away – in other words, they didn't like nosy kids! There were many whispered conversations behind closed and barred doors, with a chair jammed under the doorknob, and he found it difficult to hear what was going on behind the solid panels. Several times the little espionage agent landed on his face when the door was very quickly opened. It puzzled him at the time why they should all be so secretive.

Anyway, his brother Cliff had got out of a very sticky situation, and without Hardy Flower's help. The second young lady, Win, remained for the rest of the week, while the other young lady Pat went on her way, having been 'given the elbow'.

Cliff's new girlfriend was an exceptionally good cook, and always cooked enough food, so that Daisy and Hardy Flower could have a feed whenever she came to Gravesend. The third of the brothers, Jim, also had a girlfriend, by the name of Jean, whom Hardy Flower thought was a very pretty young lady, although Jim and Jean's romance didn't last very long. Ken, who was in the Royal Air Force, also took his girlfriend home. Her name was Enid, and the boy brat liked her because she always brought her sweet ration and left the bag of toffees on the top of a small cupboard, quite within his reach. As pretty as Enid was, she could never understand why her sweets disappeared as quickly as they did. Hardy Flower knew, because he was the one who kept on nicking them – until there was just one left. He could never understand why Enid's face had such a nervous tick.

It was rumoured, so Hardy Flower had heard but not quite understood, that when Enid first visited Gravesend, the shapely lady of nineteen had a habit of bending forwards at the waist, keeping her legs straight and flashing her stocking tops and thighs, and usually – so the rumour continued – within their father's sight. Hardy Flower also heard that the 'bending over' of the lady was the cause of 'Baby Tim' being conceived when he was. Another Thomas family story which Hardy Flower had overheard, but didn't understand, was that he and his sister Daisy were conceived immediately after a cocktail party in the village of Ifield. Hardy Flower, thoughtful and confused, wondered why things were so complicated.

Eventually Cliff Thomas and his girlfriend Win were married, but, unfortunately, within the year Cliff had to go abroad with his army unit.

The Germans had developed two new secret weapons, called the V-1 and the V-2. The V-1 was a huge winged bomb with a rocket attached to it. It weighed one ton, and great jets of flames shot from the tail end, giving it its nickname – the 'doodlebug'. Another name was the 'buzz-bomb'. The approaching sound of the flying bomb was very distinctive, and nobody could mistake the heavy purr or buzz as it headed in their direction. This people found very frightening because all the time they could hear the buzzing purr they were safe, but when the purr stopped the bomb would start to glide downwards, to explode on impact, causing many deaths and injuries. The Spitfire squadrons sometimes flew alongside the 'doodlebugs', touching wing tip to wing tip, in an attempt to turn the rocket bomb back towards the English Channel. Sometimes they were successful, but still there were many people who got killed.

The V-2 was still more devastating. You didn't see it or hear it until it was right overhead. There was a sudden 'whoosh', followed by an almighty explosion. There weren't too many V-2s which hit Gravesend, but the few that did made life very frightening for the inhabitants.

Hardy Flower saw many 'buzz-bombs', and always wondered where they would land. Kent took the brunt of many of the bombs and the county well earned its nickname, 'Bomb-Alley'. The total number of 'doodlebugs' which fell over Kent was 2,400. London had about 2,200. And there were approximately 1,000 shot down into the sea at Folkestone. Hardy Flower tried to keep a tally by counting those reported in his dad's newspaper each day. He wasn't far out. After the final deluge, a total of 8,000 'doodlebugs' were dropped on to Kent, Surrey and London combined. It was all quite devastating. He and his mates at school thought they would be quite safe if they crept underneath the oval raffia mats which they used for their games lessons.

As the rocket bomb raids became more frequent, the more everybody became frightened and scared. So it was then that more and more children were destined to wear the evacuees' label pinned to their collar. Of course, once again the evacuation included Daisy and Hardy Flower – this was the fourth time. This time, though, they were more exclusive – they didn't have to wear labels for this journey because they had their own personal evacuee deliverer.

The twins' new sister-in-law, Win, had made several visits to Gravesend, from her home town of Darlington, which lay in the then very far-off north-east of England. So it was on one of her visits, while Daisy and Hardy Flower ate a 'special' tea to soften the blow, that they were told that they would be going back to Darlington, to live with Win and her family, which consisted of her mother, three brothers and a lodger. It was to be a nice 'holiday' for the twins, a holiday that would last 'until the end of the war'! In other words, they were being evacuated again – for ever?

At the time nobody had any idea just how long the war would last, whether England would win or lose it. Either way, it could last for months, or even years.

Win was a very kind young lady, and whenever she was cooking Daisy and Hardy Flower always got a good taste. More often than not, they would get a helping of whatever culinary enterprise Win had undertaken, whether it was breakfast, dinner or tea. And, much to their delight, Win had an extraordinarily sweet tooth. Hopefully now they'd get those treats very often!

It was halfway through 1944. Thousands of Yanks had invaded England to help out, and the Allies were about to invade Normandy, so it was fitting that Daisy and Hardy Flower were off to invade Darlington. The twins, once again, were off on another 'adventure'. Little did they realise that it wasn't going to be an 'adventure' at all. Indeed, Hardy Flower would see it as another 'trial'.

When the twins eventually arrived at Darlington, they were novelties to the harsh-speaking people of the north-east, for whom the twins were 'Cawckneys' or 'Lon'den'ers' from 'doon sooth'. Due to their south-eastern accents, however, the inhabitants of Darlington considered the twins 'posh', which was certainly a sudden turn-up for the books! What the children did enjoy was both Win's and her mum's cooking. Both mother and daughter, being excellent pastry cooks, made full use of the extra two weeks' worth of rations. Life for Daisy and Hardy Flower Thomas was going to be a lot different – as they would soon find out, much to Hardy Flower's detriment.

The day after they arrived, the twins went straight into Harrowgate Hill Junior School, which was situated at the end of the very long road they were going to live in, right in the heart of Darlington's industrial district, with its steelworks, railway engineering firms, heavy construction, and a soap works which would stink to high heaven when the wind was in the right direction.

For the twins, Harrowgate Hill Junior School was just the same as the school at home – there were 'well-off' kids and there were 'poor kids' – though, like it or not, they all had to see the 'nit nurse'. One young roughneck, a friend of Hardy Flower's, had a seemingly 'posh' girlfriend who, despite her neat and tidy appearance, had a nest of nits breeding in her blonde and plaited hair. The unfortunate incident didn't deter the young lad – he still waited for her after school and walked her home amidst the unkind catcalls. This lovely young posh girl, like the twins had had to many times before, had to walk home with gentian-violet nit-killer staining her hair.

The twins' education didn't last for very long at the junior school because suddenly it was the summer holiday, during which time Daisy and Hardy Flower had their eleventh birthday, which meant both of them being elevated to a senior school and separated. They enjoyed the school holidays because there were no air-raids to worry about, and they were getting three meals each day. They both made some new friends: Daisy's friends were from the average clean and neat families, whereas Hardy Flower's friends were from the roughshod families. On the odd occasion, and to his surprise, some of Daisy's school girlfriends knocked on the front door, quite on their own, to see whether Hardy Flower would go out to play with them, or go for a walk. The tall and skinny gawkish kid felt embarrassed because he'd never had girls knocking on the front door for him before. His attraction might have been because, at the time, he wore knee-length trousers, which were the fashion at home, but seemed to be unheard of in the north-east of England.

The new friends of Hardy Flower's were neighbours from a few doors along the street. The first lad's name was Johnny Milne, and he and Hardy Flower were much the same in their build and ways. Johnny Milne was Hardy Flower's 'best mate' all the time that the kid from 'dahn sarf' stayed in Darlington. John's family were rough, hard up and honest. Johnny and Hardy Flower were very friendly with another family, who had lots of kids, and they, too, lived a few doors down the street. Their name was Cahouny. The eldest boy's name was Tommy and he was the same age as Johnny Milne and Hardy Flower.

Hardy Flower thought his parents' house had been untidy, until he saw the Cahounys' house. The house which they lived in was, literally, a dump. The furniture, what little there was of it, was in pieces, the upholstery was in tatters, and the old-fashioned settee springs were sticking out and exposed. And the whole place stank of urine, from babies, cats and dogs. The wallpaper hung down in shreds from the walls, and over the mantelpiece the wall was black with smoke, from the coal fires. The remains of the ashes and cinders from the fire were piled high all round the fireplace.

Even Hardy Flower looked on in disdain. Not only did the place stink, it was also rotten, with lots of extra uninvited and hungry guests. Fleas and nits swarmed on the kids, the cat and the dog. But the boys, didn't care about that because they could go into the house and run amok, until Win forbade him to 'go in there', although that didn't stop the kids playing together in the streets, to sneak back into the house later when it either rained or if there was food about.

The three boys got on well together. Hardy Flower, in his short 'southern' trousers, was skinnier and almost a head taller then his new-found friends, while they were stockier and wore long trousers. The one thing they had in common was that none of the boys had fathers to guide them, so, of course, they made their own rules, which, in turn, got them many good hidings from the petticoat brigade.

Tommy Calhouny's mum was always hard up, and when the sweet ration coupons became valid each month, she always sold them to Win, who, as we know, had an extremely sweet tooth. Tommy's mum had many American service friends, who seemed to make quite a lot of visits to the 'flea-pit', the name some of the more unkind neighbours gave her house.

On either side of the house where the twins stayed at Harrowgate Hill were two families of a very dubious nature. Both families kept a very low profile, but not much could be hidden from the ever-enquiring eyes and mind of one Hardy Flower Thomas. Quite naturally, children have very perceptive minds however much things are hushed up, and didn't Hardy Flower want to be a special agent when he grew up?

The neighbours on one side seemed to be very shy and furtive, always ducking and diving out of sight when anybody appeared. There were three adults and three children. The man of the house was short and fat. He had no neck, and it seemed that his ears were on his shoulders. He continuously wore a greasy black flat cap, a shirt without a collar, and a black knotted muffler. The bottom of his waistcoat was always unbuttoned because of his huge stomach. A large leather belt, with a large flat brass buckle, held up his baggy-kneed trousers, which stopped several inches above his hobnailed boots.

The old lady was always dressed in black – black dress, black shawl, black bonnet, and black button-up boots. Hardy Flower only ever saw her twice. The third adult was a fat female replica of the old man, dressed, of course, in a greasy soiled grey-and-white gingham dress. He and she looked like twins and both wore thick horn-rimmed spectacles, with lenses so thick, they gave the impression that their eyes were popping out of their sockets.

The three children of that black and sombre household were aged twelve, eleven and ten. The middle one was the daughter, and, just like her mother, she had lank, straight black hair, and wore the same style of thick, horn-rimmed spectacles.

The secret which they hoped to keep from everybody was that in the house there lived four generations of a family. The old lady, and her son, his daughter, and her three children. Those children were not aware that their dad was also their grandfather and that their mum was also their sister. Despite this set-up, father and daughter were quite happy. The children were never allowed to play with other kids, although the other kids didn't mind because they all thought that the family who dressed in black were weird.

On the other side of the Quakers, the neighbour was a tall, matronly and blousy blonde, also with three children. Her husband was a prisoner-of-war, and he had never seen his three-year-old daughter; in fact, his other daughter had only been just a year old when he had been captured. The eldest child was a lovely-looking boy of about nine or ten, and like his mum, his hair was a mass of blond curls. The bonny lad's name was Billy, and was always referred to as 'little blond Billy'. Everybody loved the grubby, rosy-cheeked little lad, who always seemed to be running errands for his mum, if and when she was in – although it was rumoured that his mum always seemed to be out enjoying herself, or so said the gossips.

Over a certain period of time, again, according to the gossips, her clothes got bigger and looser, as she gained extra weight. There had been many nosy parkers who had several times noticed a well-known backstreet surgeon, plying her illegal profession at the house. The 'proddin' an' a'pawkin' with a knittin' needle' was performed, the scandalised neighbours said, while 'little blond Billy' peered round the curtains of his mum's bedroom window – just in case a stranger walked through the front gate. It was noticeable to the neighbourly nosy parkers that the back door and rear gate were always left open for the 'surgeon' to do a quick runner.

After those visits, the blousy blonde wouldn't be seen for a few days. It was even rumoured that 'a bairn had been born in'ter a boocket' and buried in the garden. Hardy Flower saw and heard 'little blond Billy' rush up to a neighbour, screaming out:

'Me mam's sent me, and to say she's ill a'gen, and she's bin sat on a boocket all'er night, an' could yen coom quick, lak? Ther's 'ell-uv'a mess, missus!'

'Little blond Billy's' big appealing blue eyes always won their hearts, and the neighbour took his hand, saying, 'Aye, yoong Bill'eh, ah'l coom along direct'leh, ye'r poo'r bairn! 'As the doctor been't see ye'r mam yet, soo'n?'

Blond Billy's huge blue eyes radiated complete innocence as he looked up and answered: 'Nay, me'h mam ses it's too lea't, and not ta'e ge'r a doctor. He moosn' see her in tha' stea'te. Could ye'r coo'm quick, lak? she said!'

To another neighbour, the neighbour whispered over her shoulder: 'Soo'nds lak this'un'll gaw doon the lavvy. She'll never ler'n, doo's she? No wonder they call her the cut-cloth-rug. She had just as many prods and pokes as our'n! Coom on, yoong Billie lad, let's get ye're mam sor'ed out!'

Perhaps it was spiteful gossip. As the very street-wise Hardy Flower reflected, the mums in the north, although well away from the bombing and the Blitz, seemed to be hard and bitter compared with the more sunny-natured mums of the south-east, who faced up to the bombing with a good sense of humour and took everything in their stride. 'But,' thought

Hardy Flower, 'here, or at home, their wedding-ring fingers don' 'alf hurt my head and ears when they belt me, just as much as each other's!'

12

1944–1945, Living with the Quakers

Darlington, to Hardy Flower Thomas and his sister Daisy, seemed as far away from home as the moon, and for the twins the fifth year of the war was as bleak and hard as the town's Quaker inhabitants. According to custom, the Quakers had a very strict lifestyle. The working-class men were strict timekeepers at work, and especially for the opening times of the working men's clubs and pubs during the evenings and especially at the weekends. The women stayed at home, usually in or near the kitchen range, baking their bread and fancy fruit pies, for their husband to take to work for their 'bait'.

Over their Sunday-lunch pints of Vaux Bitter and Newcastle Brown Ale, feeling refreshed after the weekly bath and a change of underwear, the Quaker men shuffled their dominos and boasted about how clever 'the little wife' was at home.

In the select part of the spit-and-sawdust alehouse, the boilermakers sat ramrod straight. They, like the ordinary workmen, wore their whitest shirt and striped or polka-dot tie, but not for them their Sunday best suit – their elevated status as boilermakers required them to wear their Sunday waistcoat, over which they wore a regular blue boiler jacket and trousers, their working 'suit'. The more the dark blue was laundered, the paler the blue, and the higher their status became. The boilermakers were a society unto themselves, and everything was a 'closed shop', which in turn made the elite tradesmen sit aloof from all others.

When those specialised and snobbish 'engineers of everything' were pointed out to Hardy Flower Thomas, little did he realise that one day – indeed, within ten years – he would be one of them.

When the Quakermen finally came out of their 'men only' spit-and-sawdust alehouses, their bladder filled to bursting with the icy chemical beer, they went home for lunch. It was love and kisses all round, before they tackled a massive Sunday roast, cheeking their 'missus' and slurring out their affection for the bairns. The mood changed hours later when, having slept off a boastful ten pints of bitter, the typical working-class Quaker man would threaten 'ter brae yer bluidy 'ead off,' as he swung a brass-buckled heavy leather belt in the nearest kid's direction. The bairns would disappear as they dodged the heavy buckle-end of their father's waist belt and once again the Quaker man would be restored to quietness. At work the next day, he'd ruminate: 'Well-aye-mun! Ah 'ad ter tek-it owt t'missus 'n bluidy bairns!'

The gang at Albert Road School was led by a bully-boy named Joss. He was a tall, thin and mean-looking boy, with a lot of cronies who toadied round him, especially another kid who came from the Isle of Wight. He, too, was an evacuee, but he had two things in his favour: he was allowed a substantial amount of pocket money, and he didn't have a 'London' accent. He called everybody 'Tosh' until eventually it became his own nickname.

To Hardy Flower, the hardbitten working-lass school seemed quite hostile. At home, his family were poor, but in the working-class area of Darlington it was a hard life all round. He was shown the three-mile walk to the school just once by his sister-in-law's brother, Jack, then left at the door of his new classroom. Very timidly, he knocked on the door and walked in. It was obvious straight away that Hardy Flower Thomas wasn't going to be made very welcome. There was a stunned silence as the skinny, half-starved kid in short trousers stood waiting for the teacher to tell him where to sit. But that was just the start of it.

For one thing, Hardy Flower's short trousers brought forth gales of laughter, from both pupils and teacher, who, when the hilarity died down, eyed him up and down with suspicion in his eyes.

'Ah! Thee ee'vac'u'ee from the war zone. Reet, lad, sit there, in the froont raw – where Ah can kep an eye on you, and see what you are made of!' Then, with a sneering smirk, he added, 'We don't have wars here!' As if war was a contagious disease from the south.

In the front row, Hardy Flower was 'on the spot', with his back to the very amused class. His problem, from then on, was to try and understand their 'foreign accent'. For instance, 'aye' meant yes. 'Oh no' sounded like 'Ee-naw!' 'Ha'way' meant 'come on! A packed lunch was 'bait'. A young girl was 'ouw'er lass.' 'Bairns' were young children. 'Ouwer kidder' was any younger member of the family. 'Teahtis' were potatoes. Money was referred to as 'a bit of silver' or 'a copper or two'. Coal to the southern kids sounded like 'ca-awl' and Mum was 'Mam'. Of course, Hardy Flower's 'foreign accent' was strange to them too, which might have accounted for their hostility.

His first rough and tumble at the school was during the first lunch-break. He got an early warning of the trouble ahead during morning playtime, when the sneaky kid from the Isle of Wight called out to Joss, the biggest and lankiest kid there:

''Ere, Joss, look at the Cockney kid; he's wearing short pants!' There and then, every kid in the playground stopped and stared. Hardy Flower stood quite alone, very startled by the sudden and threatening laughter of the other kids. When they laughed, he laughed with them, hoping that the ice had been broken. Then the bell was rung, signalling the boys to return to their classrooms, but, as they trooped into the school, Hardy Flower heard the bully-boy Joss whisper:

'We'll get the 'Cockney' kid at 'dinner-time!'

Sitting in the front row, in the Victorian classroom, Hardy Flower was constantly reminded about what was going to happen to him during the next break. His stomach ached, and he daren't ask to leave the room, not knowing where the lavatory was. His mouth was dry and he was sweating.

Dinner-time arrived, and out into the playground the boys ran, with their sandwiches, and all the time Hardy Flower hoped that the threats were just a joke. But it wasn't. Suddenly he heard several voices sing out in unison:

'OK! Scrag the Cockney kid!'

Then Hardy Flower was well and truly 'scragged' in the schoolboy fashion. He had never been roughed up like this before. Both his shirt and trousers were ripped and torn as he was kicked and punched, scratched and pinched. Hardy Flower wanted to cry – oh yes, how he wanted to cry his eyes out, but pride or perhaps fear stopped him. Instead of crying, he began to retaliate as best as he was able. The northern kids were rough and relentless, and Hardy Flower went down under their sheer weight and numbers, to be suddenly left like a discarded sweet bag – crumbled and squashed, or, in his case, bruised, scratched and bleeding.

So it was then that whenever the hostile boys needed a scapegoat, or someone to bully, it invariably was 'the kid from the souwth'. And the instigator was always Tosh. But, of course, the teacher could only blame one person for causing a fight among the pupils – Hardy Flower.

By the end of September the novelty of Daisy and Hardy Flower being 'the twins from the south' and 'the Cockney kids', or 'the Londoners' had worn off, and they both had to fall in line with the other kids. Having 'run the gauntlet' at Albert Road School nearly every day, Hardy Flower thought that the ideal thing for him would be to wear long trousers, and so become 'one of the lads'.

'Aye! Harrdy Flow'er, agreed the twin's sister-in-law. 'Yeh

could, but, if yeh want long trousis, then yeh can get che'sel' out and earn the mon'ey to peay fer'rem!'

There was only one way for the now 'go it alone' kid to earn some money, and that was 'for him to gerr'out in'ter teahtie fields and do some "teahtie pickin".'

Johnny Milne decided that he, too, would like to earn some money and together he and Hardy Flower decided to 'ger' themselves out to the farm and chance their luck – and 'ter tell the farmer yer just about ter leave school and yer need a job!'

So Hardy Flower and his pal Johnnie Milne set out to walk the five miles to the potato fields.

At the end of a morning's walk, they found that they were in luck – they could 'start at seven o'clock the next maw'nin, – daw'nt be bluidy leahte! Ye'll be workin' alongside o' grown men and grown men's work is what I want out o'yer!' Which meant that for one week, Hardy Flower and his pal Johnny Milne would have to get up in the early hours of the morning at six and walk three-quarters of a mile to catch a tram to Darlington Marketplace, where they'd queue up, hoping to get on a bus to take them to the potato fields, which were situated just over the county border into North Yorkshire. The unfortunate thing was that the buses were always full of old men, who coughed up their lungs when they lit their first cigarette. The smoke was so thick on the buses that it gave the two young boys a sore chest and throat for the next week.

It was still dark when they arrived at the farms where they had to queue up to collect a large heavy wicker basket each, and once they had got their basket, it meant they were on pay and had to start grafting.

The tractor set off, turning the heavy cold clay over, and with any luck, digging the 'teahties' out, but the clay was heavy, very wet and extremely cold. Very often, the boys would have to dig the potatoes out with their bare hands, if they were still half buried. On their hands and knees they dragged the heavy wicker baskets through the clay, banging their knees, elbows and knuckles against the frozen clay.

As they picked the clay-covered potatoes and put them in the basket, the two skinny boys moved forwards behind the tractor, dragging the basket along with them. When it was full, they had to drag it to the lorry where they heaved it up over the tailboard to get it weighed and emptied and then take it back again. They were expected to keep up with the men and the tractor all the time. It was children doing men's work, Hardy Flower in his short trousers and a small jacket, and his pal Johnny Milne wearing just a thin shirt, hand-me-down trousers and his mother's discarded high-heeled shoes with the heels knocked off. For the two eleven-year-olds, the mornings were extremely cold and bleak out in the fields.

Hardy Flower and his pal worked for one week doing a man's job, for half a man's 'teahtie-picking' wage, but Hardy Flower earned enough money to buy himself a pair of long trousers and a 'lumber jacket', which all the kids wanted at the time. His 'wages' didn't equal one pound. But he had worked hard for the trousers and he hopefully imagined: 'Now I can be one of the lads, at school.'

Johnny Milne, who for some reason attended a different school from Hardy Flower, used the money he earned to buy a second-hand pair of studded boots, and at the end of the following week his mother was showing off a new top-coat.

Hardy Flower's new trousers were thick grey serge, with turn-ups, and the lumber jacket was a chocolate-brown corduroy. They would keep him warm in the cold and bitter winter which was guaranteed in the north-east. They were the only clothes that he possessed anyway, and every weekend he religiously folded the trousers and placed them neatly under the mattress of the bed to keep the creases in until Monday morning school.

The first time he wore them, the tall, skinny but forever

162

smiling, loner walked the three miles to Albert Road, but for once didn't play about under the railway bridges, near the Whesso Iron Works, or splash around on the edge of the River Skern. Hardy Flower strutted into school in good time, so that he could enjoy the comradeship of the other lads who had been hostile towards him.

Hardy Flower was tall, especially in comparison to the northern lads, which could have made them jealous or resentful of him. As the kids came into the playground, he greeted them with a 'Hello' or a 'Wotcha' or whatever the kids said in those days, but once again he was disappointed, for he didn't get any answers, just a few grins and whispered sniggers. Then as they moved into line, Hardy Flower overheard the sneak from the Isle of Wight shout out: 'Oi Joss! the Cockney has got new trousers on!'

When Hardy Flower heard that, he thought to himself, 'I'm one of the lads now!' Then he heard the bully-boy Joss say something to his toady, as they filed into the class-room. It wasn't long before the sneak came over to Hardy Flower with the message: 'We're gonna get'cher at playtime!'

Hardy Flower's heart nearly stopped, he wanted to cry out, and say, 'Let's be friends.' But all he could hear was the sniggers up and down the rows of desks and chairs. The apprehensive evacuee dreaded the coming playtime. It seemed to him that all his efforts to be friendly had fallen on stony ground. When the bell sounded for the morning break, Hardy Flower hung about in the classroom, but the observant teacher, well aware of the kid from 'dahn sarf's' plight shouted out:

'Get outside boy! You are not supposed to be in here! Go on! Get out!' Hardy Flower went out, stepping through the doorway into the playground and feeling very much like a condemned man, and once again his stomach ached. Then the dreaded boy from the Isle of Wight spoke.

'Joss wants to see you. He wants to talk to you.'

This was said in a very friendly manner, but Hardy Flower was warily hesitant. The toady spoke again.

'Come on. You'll be OK now.' It sounded like a genuine promise.

Hardy Flower's heart gave a leap, as he thought, 'This is it! I'm one of the lads now!'

Suddenly, though, without any warning, he took the brunt of the full gang as he turned a corner of the building. It seemed as if they were out to do him some real harm, all pulling and tugging, some punching and some kicking. Hard leather boot soles crashed into his shins as fists crashed into his back and he screamed weakly as a punch reached his kidneys making him want to vomit, but a brutal knee hit his crotch, cancelling out the previous pain. Once again, there seemed to be no end to the physical abuse which he had to suffer almost daily. He felt the salty taste of blood running into his mouth from his nose which felt twice its normal size and most definitely out of its original position – the battered boy was sure it was broken. Suddenly he was allowed to stand up, and as he blinked away the tears he heard more catcalls and sniggers, but even before he could clear his eyes free of tears, he was given a hard shove which sent him sprawling into several other boys, who in turn pushed him forward.

More tears filled Hardy Flower's eyes, blinding him in his anguish as he was shoved round and round the circle to 'run the gauntlet'. The fists, knees and boots might only have belonged to boys twelve years old, but the kids' bullying anger added impetus to their animalistic and evil urges. Hardy Flower was saved by the end-of-playtime bell, and as the shoving stopped, he fell, aching all over, broken-spirited and sniffing as the kids ran off to get into their class lines. His shirt was hanging out, some of the buttons had been torn from his new lumber jacket, and his brand-new trousers were scuffed, muddied and wet.

A tall thin figure loomed over the cowering boy, and instantly his mind and body prepared themselves to take another beating. As Hardy Flower looked up, a familiar voice snarled:

'Get up boy, and get into line!'

Hardy Flower did as he was told, and for some reason which he couldn't understand, there seemed to be an element of satisfaction in the playground. How he wished that he was going home, just to get into some mischief, and take a couple of double-handers from his dad. He wouldn't have minded the air-raids or going hungry again – it would be worth it.

Although the physical attacks against him gradually died off, Hardy Flower had many more playground skirmishes and rough-houses during the next year and he had to except the fact that he was on his own, and not 'one of the lads'. The clothes which he had worked hard for and fought over were to last him through the next eleven months while he lived in the North-East, without any washing or cleaning, and then a further year when he returned home.

One thing about Albert Road School, it was more advanced than Hardy Flower's school at home. With their northern accent and different methods of teaching, he didn't have a clue as to what they were trying to teach him, especially in the science class, because nothing at all registered in his brain. Hardy Flower didn't realise that for some unknown reason he was up against the kids, the teachers and the system.

He was the loner, a victim of circumstance. One incident, most definitely put the head teacher's back up. Outside the school door, facing the other half of the school across the road, was an iron gateway, with a short wall on each side of the gate pillars. The walls were just long enough, and high enough, for Hardy Flower to sit on. As most boys at some time or other go through a spitting phase, making them feel bigger and older, so did Hardy Flower. One day he was sitting on the wall feeling sorry for himself as he worked up a mouthful of saliva, thinking that if he was a good 'spitter', he could make some friends at school. The neighbours' kids were neutral at school, possibly for their own safety. The saliva was ready, he had a good mouthful of well-churned and frothy spit, but what to do with it? However, Hardy Flower decided to try for 'distance', so, working his cheek muscles, and with a mouthful of air for power, he spat as hard as he could. However, not being a practised 'spitter', the mouthful of froth didn't go very far. It travelled straight towards the middle of the gateway step, and there, much to his horror, it landed right on top of the headmaster's highly polished boot – just as he was going to visit the other half of his school.

The headmaster looked first at his boots, then at Hardy Flower's stricken face, then back to his splattered boot, and slowly and with utter disgust, he roared,

'You filthy little swine! ... You product of the gutter! What do you think you are doing?' Then, the hatchet-faced headmaster's eyes lit up as he roared: 'Aha! The ee'vac'u'ee, Harrdy Flow'err Thomas! I might have guessed it! You're the wretched troublemaking lout from the south! Come with me this instant!' Hardy Flower had made the headmaster's day.

The tall and skinny kid had no choice in the matter, as the jubilant teacher grabbed him by his ear, making him walk on his toes as he dragged the now very wretched boy through the classrooms by his stretched ear. In the headmaster's study, Hardy Flower received a 'sound thrashing', still held by his ear as the psyched-up thrasher of boys forced the luckless lad over a bony knee. Grabbing a short thin cane, the headmaster swished it up and down to give Hardy Flower six of the best, knocking the dust from the seat of the boy's new trousers. It did absolutely nothing for the lonely boy's morale, his ego or his ear, not to mention his very sore bottom.

Hardy Flower hated the school, and everybody in it. He couldn't do anything right, or even do anything about it. How he wished that there was a friendly man whom he could be friends with, and he wouldn't even have minded an occasional swipe round the face. How he wanted to cry his eyes out, but there was nobody to go crying to.

13

' 'T'wasn't me!'

The weather became colder and very bitter as the winter settled in. Tommy Cahouny, Johnny Milne and Hardy Flower often went to the cemetery, a hundred yards along the road from where they lived. Among the tombstones they'd look for a newly dug grave out of which they could scoop some soft clay. Then they would sit and mould the clay into 'hand warmers', which was nothing more than a clay box with a funnel at one end and a small breather-hole bored into it at the opposite end to let the air in. The fuel for their hand-warmers was a piece of smouldering cloth, which baked the clay hard and warmed their hands. They needed something to keep them warm because they weren't allowed in any house before teatime, except in Tommy's extremely grotty and flea-ridden place. But the tallest and skinniest of the three, Hardy Flower, was forbidden to go in there, because he had already caught head-lice and fleas from his grubby, crop-headed friend.

On a very cold and dark night, as all the shops closed at six o'clock, Hardy Flower was sent to an off-licence which was about a half a mile for him to walk through a park, alongside the local cemetery, and finally through a wooded copse. He felt so frightened that he decided that he'd use his sister-in-law's old bicycle without asking. But unfortunately for him it had no lights – back or front. Undeterred, the now-crafty and devious boy took the bike and set off, but, unfortunately again, both back and front tyres were flat, causing the wheel rims to grind horrendously over the cobbled back alleys. Not to be defeated, he decided to carry on and half carried the bicycle out of earshot of the house. It was hard going up the hill in the pitch dark, and because of the war and the blackout, even that far north nobody was allowed to shine any lights.

Puffing and panting with the effort, Hardy Flower reached the top and started to grind the wheel rims into the road. At that point the bicycle seemed to want to go its own way as he realised that he was hurtling through the trees at the edge of the park ... then ... kerr'rash! The front wheel hit a tree, and the rider sailed up and over, to end up sitting in the dark, wondering what had happened ... where was he? When he realised where he was, he was up and away, hastily grabbing and dragging the bicycle to get away from the big red-bricked house with turrets which, according to local legend, was the most haunted house in Darlington. For a dare, Hardy Flower had visited and searched through every room in the house, quite unaware of its reputation. In the middle of this act of bravado, his two pals, Johnny and Tommy, crept through the garden and threw bricks through the windows, shouting out their ghostly wails.

Hardy Flower hid the old bicycle behind a hedge and walked the rest of the way to the shop to get the goods, then on the return journey he dragged the mangled heap back to the house. Both the wheels had been extremely buckled and several spokes were missing. It wasn't his night.

The written-off lady's bicycle lay there for several weeks before it was noticed, but, of course, when Hardy Flower was eventually asked about it, he just answered: 'T'wasn't me!', pretending that he didn't know a thing about it. 'After all,' he thought, 'that was then and it's history.' Nobody believed him for one minute and under extreme pressure, he conceded that it might have been him. That, of course, was considered to be an admission of guilt, but fortunately he was let off.

Fish and chips being very cheap, it made a welcome and tasty supper which most working-class families indulged themselves in most nights. 'Chips and fish!?' Hardy Flower always enjoyed them at any time, but at his home in the south-east only the grown-ups were allowed fish and chips. One star-lit evening, Hardy Flower sneaked into Tommy Cahouny's house, where Tommy's mum, a lady generous both in her proportions and her liberality with her affections, was doing her bit for the war effort by entertaining her American soldier lover. She suddenly thought that he might like some supper. In other words, Tommy and his evacuee friend from near London were in her way, so she sent them off to the fried fish shop. It was a frosty and bitter night and the two boys, like most working-class kids, didn't have any extra clothes to keep them warm. Hardy Flower and Tommy were not very well clothed at the best of times, so gloves, scarves and caps were not for the likes of them. If they complained of the cold, they were told to 'run about to get warm, and not to be so bluidy soft!'

So off to the fish shop they ran, and as usual there was a queue, and while they waited they got hungry, as the aroma of fish and chips drifted up their nostrils. Having been served with 'cod 'n' chips' – twice for Tommy's mum and her American lover, the two cold and hungry kids started their walk home. But on the way home, Hardy Flower decided that he and Tommy deserved a taste of the mouth-watering cod 'n' chips which had been well salted and vinegared. The scalding-hot battered fish had made the newspaper wrapping very wet and soft, so posed no problem for Hardy Flower's very grubby and probing fingers!

He and his friend Tommy Calhouny tucked into the delicious battered cod with such relish that, by the time they got near to the house, Tommy felt quite concerned that they had eaten at least half of the wrapped-up supper. Tommy was frightened and whispered to his pal who usually had an answer to everything:

''Ee! Wha' can Ah seay abouwt this big haw'l in the caw'ner of the wrappin' peah'per?'

Hardy Flower's hardened survival instinct gave him an immediate answer. 'Quick! Drag yer knee along this wall and say that yer fell over an' squashed the package when yer fell on it ... Squash it and tear it a bit more!'

Straight away, Tommy Calhouny dragged his knee along a wall, making both himself and Hardy Flower wince, Tommy in pain, and Hardy Flower at the thought of it and at the waste of the succulent cod and chips! Once the wound had been effected they squashed the remains of the fish and chips to make it all look accidental.

When they arrived back at Tommy's mum's house, they found that they had been locked out, but after several minutes of frantic banging on the door knocker, the door was finally unlocked by Tommy's Mum and frantically the boys both quickly told her about his 'accident' in the blackout. The sight of his knee convinced her that Tommy had really hurt himself. The scratches and cuts were quite deep and were bleeding profusely. Of course, both the lip-licking brats got a lot of sympathy from Tommy's mum, as well as some candy and chewing gum from her Yank.

A 'tart' she might have been, untidy and slovenly, but she had a heart of gold. She clasped the boys shorn heads to her partially exposed bosom, giving them both a hug and kisses. At the touch of her warm swelling breasts, Hardy Flower's mind flashed back to the melon-like breast of his mother's friend, with its huge moist strawberry protruding from the front. It had made him blush then, but on this freezing cold winter's night and hundreds of miles away from his parents and home, the lofty twelve-year-old felt his heart begin to pound as his face was clamped between the two large soft and very warm mammaries. To his pleasant surprise, his loins became hot and his knees weakened – overcome by some unknown desire. For some yet-to-be discovered reason, he wanted 'titty' ... but Hardy Flower would meet a few more tarts like her, and at a later stage of his life he'd realise that sometimes they make the best wives, friends and neighbours. It was a pity, really, that the two boys had eaten the tart and her lover's supper, though in their defence they were cold and hungry.

In a derelict old factory, on the opposite side of the park, Hardy Flower and Tommy puffed on their very first cigarette. They always went into a derelict old building and found a hiding place to sit and smoke, and act grown-up. The old lady in the corner shop where they bought the Woodbines didn't like the two skinny and scruffy brats, so she reported them to Hardy Flower's sister-in-law. She eventually asked the two boys whether they had been smoking, which they hotly denied. However, a search of their pockets showed some threads of tobacco and their breath smelt smoky. The sister-in-law was so annoyed with them that they got a severe 'choking off'. It must have been very effective because neither of them smoked again.

During the cold and wet weather, the twins had to make a cloth rug. Although Daisy and Hardy Flower didn't know it, they were making the rug for a special reason, because, unknown to them, their parents were coming to see them and their sister-in-law and her mother thought that it would be a good idea if the twins showed that they were doing something useful.

On many occasions, Daisy and Hardy Flower met each other from their schools, usually in the local park, where they would walk and talk about how they missed being at home. They wondered how long they would have to stay, just hoping that they might go home soon. Sometimes they felt lost and left out, and not knowing where to turn, they cried on each other's shoulders. They didn't know, then, what 'waifs and strays' were, but one day they would look back and know exactly that that was how they must have felt, and probably what they looked like.

When the day arrived for their parents to visit them, the two evacuees were in for a big disappointment, because, for some unexplained reason, the visit was cancelled. Daisy and Hardy Flower had got used to disappointments in their younger days, but it went just a bit deeper that day, as they had both got very excited, and ran the several miles home from school, only to be told: 'Calm down, they've sent a telegram to say they aren't coming.'

That was it, and the twins had to wait another three long weeks, when, once again, they ran home in record time. Out of breath, they rushed into the house they called 'home' much too early and were ordered back out and to wait well away from the house.

'Come back in half an hour, holding hands and smiling!'

The twins went out and came back, only to be told to run off again, and come back in another half-hour, still holding hands and smiling. This they did but it was still too early. They were in and out like a fiddler's elbow. Again, they went out, full of misery. Eventually, they went in, fully expecting to be sent out again. Then Win suggested that they both went into the passage behind the front door, and wait for their parents there, but Hardy Flower guessed straight away what Win was up to.

'Yeah! I bet Mum and Dad are in there!'

To their delight, their parents were hiding from them. They soon discovered, though, that things seemed different. Their parents spoke 'funny', for one thing, like they all did 'dahn sarf'.

The weekend was brief, and soon over, and there were lots of tears from Daisy and Hardy Flower when it was time for their Mum and Dad to depart. The twins didn't know when they would see them again, or when they were likely to go home themselves. That's all that they could remember of the weekend, except that, straight away, Daisy and Hardy Flower had to 'get on with the rug, and stop crying!' The rug hadn't been mentioned at all during their parents' visit.

Making a 'cloth rug' was hard and monotonous when it was started from scratch. The first thing the twins had to do was to go out and collect a pile of old clothes such as jackets or skirts, the thicker the better. The next stage in the operation was to strip all the lining from the inside of the garment and put it to one side. The heavier material was then cut into strips about four inches long and one inch wide, None of the garments was washed or cleaned; some were hairy and itchy and most of them smelled of damp or mildew. Perhaps it was stale perspiration. Daisy and Hardy Flower sat and cut hundreds and hundreds of various cloth strips. The unfortunate part was, the scissors were always blunt.

A piece of hessian from a large flour sack was stretched out, and the twins made an attempt to draw a pattern on it with a piece of soft chalk. This was erased with the movement of the rug, so it had to be drawn and redrawn. For the twins, it was hard work and boring. Prod and poke, prod and poke ... it was a soul-destroying hobby as their hands became sore and tender with the constant prodding with the iron spike ... prod a hole and poke the cloth in ... prod another hole and poke the other end of the cloth in. The rug got heavier, as they worked nearly every evening on the heavy stinking material. There was no television or radio to entertain or ease the burden. When the rug was finally finished being prodded and poked, the twins' next task was to turn it over and cut every piece of strip, to make the rug look even.

The twins' sister-in-law and her mother thought the twins would enjoy making the rug for their mum, but it had taken too long to make and to Daisy and Hardy Flower, it seemed as if they were in prison and doing a stint of 'hard labour'.

"T'WASN'T ME!"

Jack, the second son in the household, was on the verge of leaving school when he did something which upset his mother. Whether it was smoking or drinking, or perhaps he was just answering her back, no one seemed to know. However, Jack must have caught her at the wrong moment for she turned on him, aiming a blow at his head, which sent him flying across the living room. The irate mother followed up by giving him such a beating that he fell to the floor, oblivious to her language which had turned the air blue. The fourteen-year-old boy lay on his side with his knees bent up to his chin in the protective foetal position with his hands covering his head. Then his enraged mother really went to town on him as she kicked and she punched, then her knee went down on to his chest pinning him down. The twins' official guardian seemed almost mad as she clawed and punched at her second of three sons with murder in her eyes. It was very fortunate for him that somebody was able to pull her away from him. Her wrath was doing the defenceless boy a lot of bodily harm.

It could have been one of two things which made the middle-aged lady run amok. The fact the she had been made a widow and lost a son both within one year, or else she was in the 'change of life', something which was openly discussed. Whatever the cause was, nobody ever found out. Jack had the worst hiding Hardy Flower have ever seen in his life, and it was no wonder that two years later, Jack joined the Royal Navy.

It was a good thing for Hardy Flower that Jack's Mum lost her temper at the time because, at a later date, Hardy Flower gave her good cause to murder him. During the war years the only ice cream which could be obtained was home-made, whipped up in the garden shed of an old Italian ice cream maker named Natriani, who would one day be the founder of a huge ice cream business in the north-east of England. Every Sunday the kids took it in turn to run to the

175

'Eye-Tiddly-Eye-Tie', and get sixpenny-worth of ice cream, which they all did quite willingly. Of course, when it was his turn, Hardy Flower dashed off thinking, 'I'll have my first share of ice cream on the way home, and the second share when everybody gets their first!'

The sacred vessel which the keen ice cream collector was entrusted with to carry the 'luxury' home in had been a family heirloom of the late Mr Harris – the twins' guardian's husband. It was a huge china pot which had passed down through the family, and well over one hundred years old.

Unfortunately, when Hardy Flower arrived at the Italian ice cream maker's shed, it was closed, owing to the old eye-tie not being able to buy somebody's war rations of milk and sugar, the ingredients he needed to make the ice cream. Back to the house Hardy Flower ran, long and skinny, like a starved praying mantis. Crossing over the busy road where they lived, Hardy Flower tripped over the kerbstone and bruised his knees. The worst part of the calamity was that he'd completely smashed the family heirloom.

'Now I'm in for it!' he thought. 'I'm bound to get some of what Jack had last week. I'll end up in a mince pie!' His mind worked overtime, as he recollected the 'Bashing of Jack' during the previous month, as well as the many thuds and thumps which he himself always managed to collect, in and out of school.

These thoughts, then, were his cue to go for his very first schoolboy Oscar. He'd tried it on with Tommy Cahouny's mum when they had scoffed the fish and chips, but surely it would be a dead cert that he wouldn't be mollycoddled by his shrewish guardian? When he picked himself up from the kerb, he did his best to look like a sad and crestfallen boy on the verge of tears and, having picked up the pieces of china, limped through the garden gate.

Astonishingly, there was some sympathy for him that day, and having earned his Oscar he was told 'not to worry about the pot'. In fact, the distraught boy was given two pieces of apple pie, first a piece from one pie, and then a piece from a second pie. Hardy Flower thought, 'It pays to put on an act!' For some reason, Mrs Harris, although she was inclined to be 'uptight' on many occasions, had started to be more lenient towards the twins in her care.

The snow was very heavy in the north-east during the last year of the war, and everywhere was frozen. If the kids had to go to the shops, they could easily drag a wooden fruit box across the ice, and it was good fun, but at school Hardy Flower, always the lone and easy target, faced a barrage of snowballs. Many times, he tried to sneak into the classroom, to avoid the hassle, only to find one or two of Joss's boys already there, waiting to give him grief.

On one occasion, he fell out with both Tommy and Johnny both at the same time. They were his two only pals, but something set them against him; perhaps Hardy Flower was feeling sorry for himself or was enraged over something, making the 'brat of a boy' in him come out. They had started pushing and shoving him and Hardy Flower thought, 'That's it! I've got nothing to lose now that my only two pals are against me – they can have some as well!'

He waded in, fists flying in all directions. Tommy and Johnny were shorter than Hardy Flower, both being slightly built and wiry, while the southern kid was like a stick insect, all arms and legs. They fought on the pavement and in the gutter, and Hardy Flower yelled:

'I'm fed up with you northern kids ganging up on me and coming in mob-handed, I'll be glad to go home where we fight fair!' But in the back of his mind was the memory of the gang at home led by a girl who carried a swish – he could almost feel the slashing pain ripping round his legs from her vindictive whipping.

Suddenly the fighting stopped, as a rival gang of kids from the back alleys came looking for trouble. Without any further ado, the three boys were pals again and immediately got stuck into their rivals. It wasn't very long before both gangs had had enough of the brawling and parted, throwing out the usual threats and taunts at one another.

'Yer!?' Yer 'an whose army!?'

'Yer!' We don't need no army – just us, on our own! Hardy Flower's bin in the war, 'e as!'

'Yer, the next time!...' The threats disappeared into the distance.

Hardy Flower, Tommy and Johnny left to engage in some other mischief with a vengeance.

In the darkness they crept along the front of the terraced houses, tying a long piece of string to each door-knocker and then on to the milk bottles which had been placed on the windowsills. Then they'd ran along the terrace, knocking on all of the doors as they passed. All the doors were opened to the boys' knock, then, one after the other, the bottles crashed on to the pavements. It was a stupid and dangerous game that deserved a severe punishment which none of the wartime brats ever received.

Winter passed into spring and, as the weather got warmer, the gang of three scruffy boys 'borrowed' unattended bicycles to go off and fish for pike. The pike were either out of season or they were trespassing, so invariably they were chased away by a water bailiff or a gamekeeper.

Occasionally, Daisy and Hardy Flower would hear how the war was going, and one day they heard the war would be over very soon, and that they could go home. It also meant there would be lots of rejoicing in the streets and in the pubs.

There were a lot of kids in the street where they lived, and when the war was over at last a big street party was organised for everybody. So, from then onwards, until the war was 'officially' over, everybody paid in one shilling for each child every week. The plan was to give all the kids a terrific time, and the adults would also enjoy a memorable evening.

The music was organised, with Tannoys set up on lamp-posts and in the trees. Everywhere was covered in coloured bunting, which fluttered in the gentle summer breeze. Everybody was getting excited, and there seemed to be electricity in the air. The weeks went by, and then came the news: the war in Europe was finally over. It was now officially 'Victory in Europe'. The people were ecstatic with joy, in the knowledge that Britain was at peace.

The date of the party was decided – it would be the following Saturday – and everybody paid a bit extra. All the busy-bodies were dashing hither and thither, and all the kids were excited and were given trivial jobs to do. Hardy Flower and Daisy helped out, too, not minding what they did. And as they prepared for the end-of-war party, adults and children were kind to the twins, talking about them going home to their mum and dad, 'yer poo'er wee bairns!' Everybody became more and more excited, but not quite as excited as Daisy and Hardy Flower.

On the day of the party, all the kids washed behind their ears for once, and even consented to have their necks washed. The boys had their hair greased and combed flat against the scalp, and the girls had a coloured ribbon in their hair instead of a wire clip. The party was getting nearer, and all the kids were all ready to go, with Daisy and Hardy Flower feeling the happiest they had been for a long, long time.

Out in the street the atmosphere was electric as the twins mingled with the other kids, until it was time to sit down for the street party. The street was divided up into sections, and their section was in a cul-de-sac shaped like a keyhole, so into the keyhole Hardy Flower and Daisy trooped as they laughed and joked with all the other kids, all trying to get in first, as they got nearer and nearer to the laid-out tables.

But at the last minute and just as they were about to sit down, it was decided that as Daisy Thomas and Hardy Flower Thomas didn't really live in the street, or belong to the area, the twins wouldn't be allowed to go to the party. The street was at least six hundred yards long. An almighty row ensued between the twins' sister-in-law and the organisers. First they were going, then they weren't going, then they were, and then finally, the sister-in-law's three brothers were allowed to go, but not 'the outsiders'.

There was no more arguing: the twins were turned away as if they were undesirable beggars, turned away from the 'The war is over!' celebration. Their sister-in-law had paid in for many weeks for the five kids in her house to go to the 'Victory' party. Again, Daisy and Hardy Flower felt like outcasts as they walked shamefaced back to the house, both of them feeling very upset. Daisy was in tears, but Hardy Flower had learned the hard way at Albert Road school that 'It doesn't pay to cry!' The twins had dressed up in their Sunday best, Hardy Flower's earned by picking out frozen potatoes in a clay potato field, and Daisy's home-made dress made from a twice-round hand-me-down.

The twins walked back to the house, walking in the opposite direction to everybody else, blushing to the roots of their hair as the oncoming children stared at the rejected evacuees going the wrong way. They went into the house and straight up to the front-bedroom window, where they stood and watched forlornly the many tables lined with joyous kids scoffing themselves silly and playing games – and all to celebrate the end of a war which they had seen nothing of.

Later, when the tired kids had been put to bed, the adults put on the smoochy music and got merry or drunk. In the darkness of the bedroom Daisy and Hardy Flower spoke of things which they had forgotten during the long year and four months they had been away from home. And in their loneliness and disappointment they both sat and cried.

14

1945, No Victory Celebration Parties for the Twins

The disappointment of not going to the street party was soon forgotten when it was known that Daisy and Hardy Flower would be going back home to Gravesend. Their sister-in-law stipulated, however: 'Yehr gorra finish the rooug fairst!' The twins made every effort to get it finished by a certain date, as a special day had been arranged for evacuees to return to their home towns.

The rug was finished and it was time to go home. Hardy Flower didn't say many goodbyes; he was impatient to get home to see his mum and dad and his baby brother, Timmy.

The Thomas twins, accompanied by their sister-in-law Win, felt very happy as the huge steam engine gave a shrill blast on its whistle as if to say, 'We're on our way!' Very slowly, the great steam engine pulled out of the vast north-eastern station, and as they came out from under the station roof it seemed to Hardy Flower that the sun was shining even brighter – just for him and his sister Daisy. Then the train gathered speed, as it hurtled its way three hundred and fifty miles towards the south-east, and home.

The further south they travelled, the more bomb damage the twins saw, and when they reached London everything looked extremely bad indeed, especially between Charing Cross and Gravesend. They saw whole streets of houses lying in heaps of rubble. Factories had been bombed and smashed to smithereens. It looked as if London and the south-east had been through an earthquake. Homes, shops and factories had been bombed and blasted beyond repair. Lounges, bedrooms and kitchens, all were open and exposed to everybody's eyes and the elements. Wallpaper and torn curtains fluttered in the breeze.

Finally, and at last, after another year and a few months away from home, Hardy Flower strode along the side entrance of their house, as proud as a peacock, with his sister Daisy close behind. At the back door they both stood together on the concrete step, both seven or eight inches taller than when they had gone away a year and four months previously, both wide-eyed and anxious as they looked towards their mum, who was standing at the kitchen sink peeling potatoes. Then, with sudden joy on their faces, the twins yelled in unison:

'Hello, Mum. We've made you a rug!'

Mrs Flower Thomas, the twins' mum, looked up as they spoke, saying half-heartedly: 'What do you want? And you can leave that' – she pointed to the home-made rug which Hardy Flower had stood on end – 'outside in the wash-house!'

The steely glint in Mrs Flower Thomas's eyes reminded the disappointed kid that what his mother had just said, she had meant, the wash-house being the outside junk hole where everything was thrown, to end up being burned under the huge iron boiler.

It had been several months since Hardy Flower had allowed himself a lone weep – he'd been to a rough and hard school and crying was soon knocked out of a boy who 'booed' – but now that the love and care he had dreamed of for so many long months was not forthcoming, he felt tears prickling at his eyes. Grabbing the heavy cloth rug, he carried it outside and dumped it in the ramshackle wash-house, then with eyes already wet and a suddenly heaving bony chest he ran to the nearby lavatory and shed his pent-up tears, the frustrated tears of a rough-and-ready boy who had learned not to cry for over a year because it was 'cissy'. How Daisy felt, her twin brother didn't know, but how he needed his mum right at that moment, for her to grab him with her wet hands – the ones that had stung his legs so many times – to hug him, and love him, and tell him that she had missed him and Daisy through all those long months. He needed reassurance that they were home again, where he could laugh and understand the language, and not be involved in fights several times a week. If only his mum had just given him one good swipe to let him know he was in his own home.

Fortunately, Mr Hardy Thomas, the twins' father, was more sympathetic when he came home from work. He kissed and hugged his twins and gave them a half-crown each to spend on whatever they wished. Mrs Flower Thomas didn't like kids very much, having lost three and borne seven. Daisy, Rose and Hardy Flower never had the same privileges as the first three sons. Their father loved kids, despite his firm hand, and he loved tiny tots, especially babies, well at least until he was caught on the wrong foot or woken up from his 'sleeping it off' session on a Sunday afternoon. Then 'every little bugger in sight copped it'.

Rose too, had returned from Devon, where she had been evacuated. There she had learned how to be a 'little lady', and had returned several days before the twins, and as their flint-eyed mother remarked, 'with airs and graces'. 'She can lose them right away!' Mrs Flower Thomas added. Rose, like her name, was of a kind and loving nature and quickly had a nice tea ready for her young brother and sister consisting of bread and jam followed by a walnut and cream cake. Hardy Flower's fingertips delved into the home-made cream when nobody was looking. Mrs Flower Thomas was too busy keeping a wary eye on her uppity daughter who had come home with her new-found manners and posh ideas.

In the nearby streets more victory parties were about to take place, much to the joy of the twins who had missed out on the street party in Darlington. As their own party got nearer, the twins made themselves known to their old friends, so as to be in on the preparations, but some of the mothers looked at the twins with disdain, saying, 'Oh no, not those two scruffy children from the next road?' Another mother chimed in with an air of authority: 'It wouldn't be fair on our children to invite them. After all, they are quite rough and seem to speak differently.' She paused then added as she looked down her nose: '...And they did keep going away on long holidays. No, send them packing!' Another mother bleated her support. 'Yer'se from the north I'd say; they're no-gooders from the north, I'll be bound!'

So once again, having been turned away from Christmas parties, birthday parties and victory parties over the six years of the war, the Thomas twins were held up to ridicule and turned away, and all through no fault of their own.

The war was over, but it wasn't straight back to school for Daisy and Hardy Flower, not until after the summer holiday period. Then they would go to their local senior school, where, once again, they would meet some of their old friends, who wouldn't understand why they spoke with another funny and different accent. The twins, once again, would have to start on a different curriculum, and would gradually re-adopt their natural accent. There came a sudden realisation in the family which Hardy Flower had known but kept to himself – from the very first day when the twins had gone off to Darlington, he'd stopped wetting his bed at nights.

Before they went back to school during the summer of 1945, they had the remainder of the summer holidays to enjoy. Their father Mr Hardy Flower was going to visit his parents in the farming village in Gloucester, so Hardy Flower asked whether he could go with him and stay with his Gran and Gramps and Uncle Tom.

The tall and skinny kid spent almost a month living in the Gloucestershire village of Whitminster, doing casual work on the farm with his Uncle Tom. He didn't get paid, but he could do anything that he wished to do. His cousin Ray, who lived in Gloucester, cycled out to the village to see his Kentish cousin, tagging on to the end of a Gloucester City Cycling Club tour. The club members had cycled fast on their low-handled racing bikes, but right behind them, with his head held high, and wearing an old-fashioned scouts hat from before the war, pedalled young Ray Godding going hell for leather on a ramshackle bike, his pedals going round four times faster than the club cyclists'. Ray had made his bike up from scrap, using a huge old-fashioned lady's bike frame and a large curved cross-bar. The club cyclists sped through the crossroads, with Ray close up in the rear, until Hardy Flower shouted out for his cousin to slow down.

The blond cousin pulled up with a jerk as the front brakes clamped against a buckle in the wheel rim, almost throwing him over the handle-bars.

With his usual broad grin, he gasped,

'Argh! Oi 'uz jest goin' ta orverr'tak' em!'

He might have done so too, if his black- and crop-haired cousin hadn't stopped him.

Hardy Flower and his cousin Ray Godding, always identical in their ways and manner, were not so different in looks either. Ray was tall, skinny and blond, while Hardy Flower was tall, skinny and dark. Both cousins were bullet-headed with their hair cropped to the skull and wore their trousers torn at the seat, commonly known as being 'scruff-arsed'. Out of the two, it was thought that Ray was their Gran's favourite grandchild, but if he was, then Hardy Flower was a very close second, because really she loved 'her two boys' both the same.

Ray and Hardy Flower were exceptionally close pals as well as being cousins. The two boys always walked down the hill to carry their Gran's fresh water from the spring near the canal, and, if it was a nice day, they'd strip off and jump straight into the canal or the River Frome. Neither of the cousins bothered with swim trunks or towels because they didn't have any. The water was very cold, but they always enjoyed it. When they'd finished their doggy-paddle, they'd climb out on to the canal bank, and brush the water off with their hands and get dressed.

Very often the one-toothed old lady would sit on the front wall, waiting for the two ragamuffins to bring back her pails of water from the spring, and just for them she would wear her best black raffia hat, secured with several huge and dangerous-looking hatpins. The three of them would then walk up to the village shop, for her to just get something for her 'two boys' and as they walked, she would whistle the tune, 'If I Was a Black Black Bird...'

The boy's Gran was a specialist at making home-made mushroom ketchup and she would send her two boys to pick 'only the horse mushrooms – with black gills' two fields away from her cottage. The mushrooms were as large as a dinner plate and easily two inches thick with jet-black undersides. Later, for their tea, the two scruffy but very healthy kids enjoyed fried gammon bacon, home-grown tomatoes and one large black mushroom. Granny Thomas would only have the mushrooms if the moon was waxing, 'because,' she said, 'when the moon be on the wane, the maggots be hungry!'

The walks round the green hedges and fields were very rewarding, as Daisy and Hardy Flower had found out a few years earlier. Ray and Hardy Flower did the same, finding all sorts of bird and animal remains, or prints and other detritus showing where they had been. They collected horsehair and horseshoes, feathers and leaves, butterflies and bugs, tiddlers and newts. Where their trophies went to eventually, nobody knew.

Uncle Tom showed them how to pluck chickens, and how

to clean and gut them. He showed them how to milk a cow properly and, as they'd watch, he'd turn and squirt the warm milk jet into their faces. But when Hardy Flower tried to milk a cow, he milked it from the wrong side, making the poor cow moo and kick the bucket over as it flicked its tail round Hardy Flower's head. He didn't try milking cows again.

He loved the smell of the farmyards, though to some people it was quite nauseating – to him, it signified life and nature and pleasure. The pigs were very large and would scramble over themselves to get to the trough for their pigswill, which really did stink, though the cousins got used to it. The pigs were enormous and bred from Gloucester Old Spots.

Uncle Tom Thomas also showed them how to walk past the big old white bull, a Chillingham Wild Bull, without disturbing it. Another time he showed them how and where to find the various poultry nests, and whether or not to take the eggs. They were mostly free-range hens, Rhode Island Reds, which were a deep reddish-brown colour. The other chickens were White Leghorns and were completely white in colour, except for their red combs. One chicken was a Speckled Wyandotte, and was black with white speckles. Its mate, the cockerel, was the worst-tempered bird on the farm. It didn't like Hardy Flower, and very often the lanky boy was seen racing for his life with the berserk bird running and screeching after him with its wings outspread as if it was about to fly. Hardy Flower had one losing encounter with the cockerel, which managed to peck a nasty gash in the back of his thigh. One peck was enough for the future Royal Marine Commando.

On their adventures, the two inquisitive boys found pheasants and partridge eggs. They listened to the woodpeckers at work on their trees as the two cousins lay chewing a blade of grass. Sometimes they would try and catch a wood pigeon for their Gran to make a pie with, but they were always too slow.

When the weather was very fine, the two boys would lie

on the grassy bank of the canal, once, that is, they had chased off the grass-chewing sheep. They'd watch the skylarks flying high up in the sky and listen to the sounds of the various insects buzzing about. They had fun chasing the jewel-coloured dragonflies, which they both collected. It was so peaceful that both of them would often doze off in the warm afternoon sunshine. Hardy Flower loved to be with his cousin Ray, but what he didn't like was the geese, who, like the cockerel, were forever trying to peck him.

Their Uncle Tom's jackdaw had flown off and didn't return. They really missed teasing the cantankerous old bird, who would squawk loudly as it skidded into flight as it escaped the two mischievous cousins. Their uncle also had a lovely old black mongrel dog named Junal. He was the only dog which Hardy Flower would ever love, but the dog got old and slow until eventually he was run over by a car and killed.

A favourite country pastime for the two cousins was to take a box of their Gran's bread crusts, then sit on a five-barred gate calling to the horses. They shouted and banged on the box to attract their favourite animals' attention. The beautiful and shining horses got to know the two boys, and sometimes they would be waiting for them, neighing in anticipation of their titbits, as Hardy Flower and Ray ambled along the country lane. Very often, the boys would see a mare and a foal galloping round the field, and when the horses heard the boys approaching, they would do a quick turn and gallop over to them. Hardy Flower's favourites were the gigantic shirehorses, which pulled the hay-wagons.

He and his cousin Ray learned how cows and mares were sired, the chickens, sheep and dogs as well, indeed anything else which bred in the countryside. They saw it all, if it was the right season.

In an old barn they jumped about in an old six-seater car. With its canvas roof down and solid rubber tyres, it looked like a small charabanc. Uncle Tom told them that it had been there since the end of the First World War and that it could be worth a fortune. In the corner of the barn was a massive big barrel which stored the vintage scrumpy cider. Ray and Hardy Flower often had a quick taste of it, which made them quite tipsy and dizzy. This, in turn, made them keep falling over in the hayloft, which they thought very funny. Very often after their cider 'binges' they would fall asleep, to eventually wake up with a headache.

Suddenly, it was time for the two boys to part company and go back to their homes. When they parted, the leaves on the trees were turning to an autumn gold, and the sun was setting earlier over the tips of the Welsh mountains. For Hardy Flower, it had been the happiest month of his young life. He wouldn't hear anything more of his cousin Ray until his Gloucester cousin was doing his National Service with the 'Glorious Gloucesters', his county regiment, during the Korean War.

At home, the twins started to prepare themselves for school, which meant that Hardy Flower's long grey flannel trousers would have to be pressed, especially after all the antics which he had got up to in the farmyard. His long trousers had never been cleaned or pressed since he had first bought them. After Hardy Flower had pressed them with a hot smoothing iron and brown paper, he had to darn his thick woollen socks, which he had been doing for himself for several years now.

Everything was ready for the twins to start at their new posh senior school, St George's Church of England Modern. Mrs Flower Thomas cast her eagle eyes over her son's efforts, but when she saw his long trousers, she spoke quite adamantly.

'You are not going to school in those!'

Having said that, Mrs Flower Thomas grabbed a huge pair of wallpaper scissors and, without any further ado, cut round the trouser legs, level with Hardy Flower's kneecaps. The flint-eyed mother of the twins stood back to admire her effort and, with a satisfied nod, added:

'There you are, that looks much better – off you go!'

And that was the end of the matter. But to Hardy Flower, his trousers didn't look better. The trousers which he had worked so hard for, so that he could match the other kids up in Darlington, had been cut down to look like knee-length shorts. What was more they didn't hang right and, not having a hem, they soon looked quite ragged as the rough scissored edge began to fray. It came as no surprise for him to discover that most of the boys at his new school were wearing new pairs of long trousers and sports coats, or even a new suit. Once again, Hardy Flower Thomas was out of place.

St George's School – Church of England – Secondary Modern. It *sounded* a nice school, and it *was* a nice school, mostly. It was modern-looking and set in the countryside, on the edge of Gravesend. The school was a single rectangular building with very wide corridors and surrounded by allotment gardens. Half of the teachers were good teachers, but the other half had chips on their shoulders. The science and maths teacher, a Mr Wurvy, believed in corporal punishment and was 'cane and knuckle happy'. Whatever they learned from him was instilled with the stroke of his cane, which he carried hidden up his sleeve. Mr Wurvy was very strict and just didn't like schoolchildren, it seemed. Both Mr Wurvy and the headmaster, coincidentally so it seemed, hardened their knuckles by tapping them along the wall, as if in tune to hummed music. The headmaster 'Old Jenko's' punishment was the ultimate in stick swishing. More often than not, the sound of 'Old Jenko' swishing his cane about to get the right balance was punishment enough – the guilty kid felt as if the tips of their fingers had already been sliced off. Nonetheless, the punishment was executed and afterwards the 'naughty kid' would return to the classroom, blowing on their bruised and battered fingers before safely ensconcing them under each armpit. 'Old Jenko' believed in letting the right hand know exactly what the left hand had just received, by slashing across one hand after the other.

Mr Packet, who taught art and drawing, was a man who made 'Whacker' Wurvy seem like a kindly vicar. Mr Packet had a high-domed head which was bald and shiny on top and he walked round tensed like a coiled spring, looking round for a boy to slap. His method was to call any culprit who had dared to so much as blink out in front of the class where the irate teacher would place his hands on the luckless boy's shoulders. Then, very gently, he would turn him to face the class, and then he used both hands to position the victim's face, left cheek uppermost. The art teacher spoke very slowly, quietly and deliberately, just loud enough for everybody in the class to follow what he was saying, then, when the boy's face was in position, Mr Packet placed his right palm on the upturned cheek, stepping back a half a pace to judge the distance, asking at the same time: 'Is that comfortable, boy?'

The luckless lad would answer, very politely of course, because he knew what was coming anyway: 'Yes thank you, Sir.'

But before he'd finished thanking his aggressor, Mr Packet's hand whipped up and down, delivering a vicious slap across the upturned face, leaving the red weals of his finger marks on his victim's face. The vicious blow always sent the 'guilty' boy flying across the room. There was the odd occasion when 'Slapper Packet' followed the first blow with another upward slap with his other hand. It paid to keep out of his way.

The third of the torturers was a teacher named Mr Ling, and Mr Ling was the worst of the three. His punishments were the same as the other two – only more so. Mr Ling taught Physical Education and English. He had, apparently, been a physical training instructor in the Royal Air Force. His hair was black and wavy and always glistened with a specially perfumed lotion. Mr Ling loved himself and he put it about that he had been a Spitfire pilot, 'one of the few' during the Battle of Britain.

For the boys of St George's School – Church of England,

191

Mr Ling had some favourite sadistic pleasures in mind with which he intended toughening the boys up. As there had been a war on, and having your own training strip was unheard of, the school gymnasium had a limited amount of rubber plimsolls and sports clothes for the pupils to wear. The luxury of trainers for the feet was unheard of. Unfortunately for the boys about to undergo the physical training, there were never enough soft shoes to go round, which meant that very often it was a case of grabbing what plimsolls you could and then swapping quickly so you got the right size. For by the time Mr Ling presented himself, everyone had to be standing rigidly to attention.

The unfortunates who hadn't been able to grab the necessary plimsolls had to train in their socks, which of course didn't suit Mr Ling. He wanted everybody suitably dressed for the occasion, and the luckless boys who hadn't been able to get the necessary strip were singled out and paraded in front of the class. It was Mr Ling's habit to carry a soft gym shoe with a rubber sole, as he walked. Had the sadistic teacher taken one shoe to ensure that at least one boy could be punished?

Once in the gym, Mr Ling would expect to see four very straight lines of boys, standing ram-rod straight, then, very casually, the tyrannical teacher walked up and down the lines inspecting the boys' PT kit. Then he'd walk up to an individual and speak to him very quietly, all the while smiling, as if he was about to do the boy a favour. As the teacher passed on, the boy ran smartly to the front of the class and stood there, knowing that his punishment was going to be one of two things.

Mr Ling, like the other teachers, positioned his victims' heads very carefully, with their left cheek uppermost. Then satisfied that the cheek was suitably placed, the gentlemanly teacher flashed his gleaming white teeth in a smile, then literally swiped the boy's face with the sole of the rubber-soled plimsoll. The alternative choice of punishment was when the torturer very gently pushed the boy into a touch-your-toes position, then swung the plimsoll across the boy's buttocks with all the might of his muscular arm. Bruised buttocks were not uncommon.

A favourite 'game' of Mr Ling's was the 'boat race'. The class was divided up into four teams in the playground, with each team carrying and at the same time straddling an eight-foot-long bamboo cane. The 'crew' had to run backwards, with the exception of the 'cox', who faced the right way and whose job was to direct the 'crew'. On the blast of the sadistic teacher's whistle, the four teams would start running backwards, towards the far end of the playground where they had to turn and run again, while Mr Ling shouted, 'Faster! Faster! Faster!' The 'boat race' was always four lengths of the playground, and was only won when two of the teams were 'sunk' by getting tangled up with another team. The downed crews sometimes ended up being dragged, scratched and bleeding, across the gritted playground. Every boy in the school hated the 'boat race' and they all hated Mr Ling, who was known as the 'Marquis de Sade'.

Another trial the boys had to endure was a compulsory boxing tournament. There was no attempt to show the boys how to box correctly; the teams and opponents were just picked at random by the teachers. Each boy had three separate fights, with three opponents, over a period of one month. The fights were always a mad flail of arms and legs until a boy went down or there was a show of blood.

Hardy Flower had lost his first fight, and it had hurt, so he didn't intend losing the second time. When his next contest came round, he had to fight a lad as tall as he was but a lot heavier. He and his opponent had always got on well together and didn't particularly want to fight each other. However, the other boy was heavy across the shoulders and very muscular, all of which disturbed Hardy Flower. Both boys stepped over the gym benches which constituted the boxing ring, neither of them wanting to hurt the other. It was the 'best of three' over three rounds. Both Hardy Flower and his pal won a round each, with the last round to be the 'decider'.

Clang! The bell sounded for the final round, and already Hardy Flower's lanky arms were flailing like the vanes of a windmill. Hardy Flower danced like he had seen the boxers do in the films, though to the onlookers he looked more like a stick insect doing the sand dance.

Hardy Flower looked at his opponent, who suddenly seemed to be twice his normal size, and the look of fear in his eyes told Hardy Flower that he didn't want to lose either. He looked bigger and stronger. 'Is he going to hurt me!?' thought the lanky lad, but self-preservation prevailed.

Hardy Flower saw his chance. They were both fighting shoe-less and his boxing opponent was wearing a pair of his father's naval sea-boot socks, which were at least three sizes too big for him. As they danced around the ring, the oversized socks flapped about like a pair of white flippers. When Hardy Flower thought his pal was coming in strong, he speeded up his boxer's dance and trapped one of his pal's socks beneath his foot. Immediately, its wearer was brought to a standstill and, taking advantage of the situation, Hardy Flower swung his gloved fist straight at his opponent's bulging Adam's apple. The blow to the throat made the boy fall on to his bottom rather sharply but, luckily for the puzzled boy, the bell sounded for the end of round three. Of course, Hardy Flower was victorious, winning the round and the fight. It was the first time that he had ever fought unfairly.

Mr Ling didn't last very long at St George's. Another one of his pleasures was to send the older girls to the window-less stock cupboard, after he had removed the light bulb, then follow them in and use the darkness as an excuse to take liberties. But he was eventually reported and was confronted by the headmaster. There was no fuss, just a discreet cover-up, and Mr Ling was transferred to another county, for the girls' sake as well as his own.

The carpentry teacher, Mr Duncan, was a good and considerate teacher, with a sense of humour. He would very often jokingly imitate the accents of lower-class types of uneducated youth, and when a boy broke wind, he would say good-naturedly: 'Who's the filthy swine who can't look after himself? The animal!'

Mr Allen, always considered to be 'one of the boys', taught them metalwork, and they liked him because there was never any aggravation. He always taught them what he thought they would like to know.

Mr Rice, 'The Gentleman Gardener', taught the boys English and gardening, which Hardy Flower always enjoyed. Mr Rice was stiff-lipped and upper-class, a 'proper-speaking toff' who expected absolute respect and got it.

Class 4B's form teacher, Mr Ellison, was not only a form teacher, but also a gentleman. He was quite strict but very fair. Whereas most of the male teachers wore sombre-coloured suits, or the usual blue or brown sports jackets with grey flannels, Mr Ellison, considered to be of a bohemian nature, wore bright and gaudy heavy-check jackets, colourful corduroy trousers, and bright Hawaiian shirts. Mr Ellison's nickname was 'The Spiv', which wasn't very complimentary. A 'spiv', after all, was the lowest type of a black marketeer or wheeler-dealer.

Hardy Flower cherished his class photo, of 'Form 3B. Saint George's School Summer 1948', which included Mr Ellison. He felt at home in the C of E school and he even enjoyed his lessons. It was in a carpentry lesson one day that he first experienced some terrific pains in his abdomen. He was creased up behind a work bench, and he suddenly thought to himself: 'Arrgh, why don't the other kids get pains like this? I never ever see any of them, doubled up in pain.' That evening he

195

mentioned his pains to his mother whose instant reply was: 'Oh, you've only got a touch of gastric flu – you'll get over it!'

For many months, Hardy Flower suffered with the excruciating abdominal pains, until they eased off as he grew into manhood. Then one night, now in his twenties, they suddenly started up again, getting worse and worse until he seriously considered cutting open his stomach with a carving knife. On the third night of his agony, the doctor's diagnosis was: 'You've had stomach ulcers, old boy, and the scars are playing you up.'

But the only pains he could remember were the hunger pains of his youth.

Leabharlanna Poiblí Chathair Baile Átha Cliath

Dublin City Public Libraries